Tales of Texas:
Short Stories
VOLUME 3

AN ANTHOLOGY OF TEXAS FICTION

brought to you by

Copyright © 2018.

Each author holds the copyrights for their individual stories. All rights reserved. This book or any portion thereof may not be reproduced or used in any manner whatsoever without the express written permission of the author(s) except for the use of brief quotations in a book review.

Printed in the United States of America

First Edition: November 2018.
ISBN: 978-0-9911435-9-7

Cover art copyright © by Colleen D'Antoni.
Except where noted, interior illustrations by Colleen D'Antoni. Book design by David Welling.
Compiled by Elizabeth Domino.

Houston Writers House
http://houstonwritershouse.net/

Foreword

TALES OF TEXAS: VOLUME 3 showcases the brilliance in a variety of stories from the Houston Writers House about the great state of Texas. This volume will be the final piece of this trilogy.

Denise and I would like to give a Texas style shout out of thanks to Elizabeth Domino, HWH Press Director, for her tireless efforts to complete these three volumes. We would also like to extend a special thanks to David Welling for his cover design work and also to the many editors who worked to make the words right especially to all the writers who were brave enough to submit to the contests and share part of themselves. A huge congratulations to all those whose pieces are a part of these three volumes. It has been a true labor of love.

We hope you enjoy your adventures in Texas and thank you for supporting the Houston Writers House and its authors!

Rebecca Nolen & Denise Ditto Satterfield

Contents

Our Gulf Coast Vacation in Leota Myer Hess' Chrysler Sedan 2
    by Steve Koch

Duke, Me & The Men in the Sheets 14
    by Curt Locklear

Ghosts of Chinese New Year 26
    by F.S. Lynch

Gunfight of the Century 42
    by Stan Marshall

Four Days in the Texas Hill Country 58
    by Mary Jo Martin

Too Darn Friendly 64
    by Jim 'from Texas' Matej

Legacy Ranch Scrapbook.. 70
    by Carol and William Mays

A Path Best Unwalked 80
    by Derpy_Girl

Time by the Sea 84
    by Kate Mock

Not So Wonderful 94

   by David Welling

Let the Grapes Grow 112
  by Janet Shawgo

West Texas Initiative 126
  by Warren B. Smith

Come Saturday Morning.. 136
  by C. Hart Palumbo

The Yellow Rose 148
  by Janet Shawgo

About the Artist

Colleen D'Antoni was raised for most of her childhood in Longview, Texas. She graduated from Spring Hill High School with numerous honors.

Her college education took place on the east coast, at Savannah College of Art and Design in Savannah, Georgia; where she earned a BFA in Illustration.

Colleen currently lives in Dallas, Texas, and aspires to continue her education in art. Though she considers herself a painter at heart and loves working in oil paint, focusing mainly on portraits; she is well versed in a variety of mediums. Her inspiration comes from various places, people, and situations. She loves spending time outside, walking her dog or cycling, and hopes to one day travel around the world.

Instagram: @c.dantoni
Facebook: C.D'Antoni

Our Gulf Coast Vacation in Leota Myer Hess' Chrysler Sedan

By Steve Koch

Our Gulf Coast Vacation

IT ALL STARTED THE DAY the wife came home with "Great News."

To myself I said, "Oh boy, now what?" To her I said, "That's great, let's hear it."

Before continuing on, I should, in all fairness, give you a few background details to set the scene for what you are about to read. It was the late 1980's in Houston; we were recently married. The price of oil had crashed, and the widespread drop in house prices had allowed us to buy our first house. Overbuy would be a better word, meaning we were house-rich and cash poor. I had already sold my bachelor car (a Porsche – that was the moment the reality of marriage really set in). We needed another car, though, and had been trying to decide what to buy.

Now, back to the "Great News." It turned out one of my three mothers-in-law - the one affectionately though privately called the "WOO," short for the "Wizard of Oz," because she was always looking for Oz but was just about never on the Yellow Brick Road – had called with a deal for us. The late Mrs. Leota Myer Hess, a casual family friend, had left a very low mileage car in her garage, which her daughter was trying to get rid of. This was "Great News" because – you know what is coming next – it had only been driven to the grocery store and the Episcopal Church and had low mileage and was in great shape.

My mind briefly went back to the apocryphal story from my youth about the guy whose elderly neighbor had an old Chevy in her garage that had been her late husband's favorite car and he could have it for $250. The Chevy turned out to be a five or ten year old Corvette Stingray (as we called them back then) and off the guy went with a "you-know-what" eating grin on his face.

But of course that was some other guy. Mrs. Hess's car was a mid-1980's Chrysler four door sedan so nondescript I would not remember what the model name was except for the fact that the wife reminded me it was a 1984 Le Baron. Nondescript in this case meant interior and exterior grey-green colors that we had not seen elsewhere before or since, a radio which quit functioning not long after it became ours, and a barely functioning air conditioning system. Suffice it to say that the hour of its production was not one of Chrysler's finest.

We were in need though, and Mrs. Hess's Le Baron became ours. After a year or so of using it to do the usual things people do in the city, we decided to drive from Houston to Orlando to meet up with my family for summer vacation. And because—believe it or not—the Le Baron was our lowest mileage and therefore expected to be the highest reliability vehicle in our stable, away we went. Packed of course with everything my Southern Belle wife needed for a trip of any length longer than, well, longer than a few hours. I did manage to squeeze in my golf clubs.

Our adventure really got started when, an hour or two after having turned over my driver duties to the same Southern Belle, I decided to wake up. Just out of curiosity I looked over at the part of the dashboard that tells one how much fuel is in the vehicle's tank. I used to call it the "fuel gauge," but that phrase must not be clear enough for some folks, so now I use more words in full sentences when asking how much fuel is in the tank.

By then we are in the middle of the Atchafalaya swamp – read alligators, Cajun good (and bad) old boys and little else – and the gauge is so far past E that I had to look four times to see if I was reading it right and then pinch myself to make sure I was awake. I was and I was, and it seemed appropriate to calmly but forcefully yell "What are you doing - you are practically out of gas!"

According to Wikipedia, the Atchafalaya is the largest swamp in the country.

The bridge crossing it is 18.2 miles long. Trust me, though, that bridge feels a lot longer when your car is breathing fumes for fuel. There is nothing visible in either direction but the aforementioned gators and old boys. One does not want to get stranded anywhere on that 18.2 mile stretch of Louisiana's finest swamp bayou country.

Luckily for us the sign for an exit soon appeared on the horizon, which we of course followed in the hope that a station would quickly be in sight. Exxon, Mobil, Shell, Chevron? Not a chance. The station's name, as I recall, was something like "Cajun Fuel and Gasoline" and then in lower case had a second billing "Specializing in Homemade Boudin" (you know, kind of like those subtitles that Rocky and Bullwinkle always had when announcing their next show, "Rocky's Summer Adventure," or "Moose on the Loose"). We limited our purchase to a tankful of Cajun gasoline— the remote setting and the good old boy attendant not giving us comfort on the content of the boudin—and we continued on eastward.

You may now be thinking all's well that ends well – we did not run out of gas in the middle of swamp country. You would be wrong.

Leota's Chrysler never, ever, ever - during that vacation or for the rest of its life – ran right again. There is nothing more to be said. It chugged, it backfired, and it hesitated. It never stopped completely - not too often anyway - but we never really knew for sure what it would do. Every trip thereafter, short or long, was an adventure.

Not long after that Cajun-fueling-up we remembered the Le Baron's air conditioning issues. In addition to having a marginal cooling capability, the air conditioner could not be on when we wanted to do what most of the world would call accelerating. For example, on a driving vacation one might want to safely merge into traffic from an on-ramp or try to pass a slow- moving vehicle. Neither were in the cards for us, although now that I think about it passing was not a problem since we were the slow-moving vehicle. In any event, our chugging and backfiring car was even more strained if we wanted to be air conditioned. Ah well, we were halfway to our destination. We would survive.

I was back behind the wheel as we made our way to Biloxi, staying the night at a casino unsuccessfully trying to win a new car. For that matter we were unsuccessful at winning anything.

When we got back in the car, still chugging, backfiring, and hesitating, we headed for Bayou La Batre, which has some sort of a family connection involving my three mothers-in-law.

I guess I have been lax in not explaining about my mother-in-law situation. You have met my first mother-in-law, the Woo, who was the middle child of three sisters. Of the other two, the youngest, the FOO, was closest genetically to my wife, being her mother. The oldest sister, the KOO, fills out the trio. The three worked together to make sure their northern heritage son-in-law kept on the straight and narrow. Wasn't I lucky? The KOO and FOO acronyms have no special meaning except for rhyming with WOO and having starting letters that match those of the names of the individuals in question. The way I talk with acronyms and such drives the wife nuts, which of course is why I do it.

You will no doubt understand that I was present for the planning of our Gulf Coast adventure but did not have an actual participatory role in the decision-making process. That is important to know as the next several stops were to revisit venues at which my three mothers-in-law spent time in their youth. From Biloxi we took the coast road, such as it was, to Bayou La Batre, a pleasant coastal spot in all regards, most of which apparently have to do with the shrimping industry. If I have the in-law family history correct they were not shrimpers and only stayed in Bayou La Batre as a final non-Texas KOO, WOO, FOO residence before moving to Houston. I guess they were not really that interested in getting to Texas as fast as they could, despite the words on the bumper stickers.

On we went to the eastern shore of Mobile Bay, where most of the very early non-Texan youth of my three mothers-in-law was spent in Daphne, the pre-Bayou La Batre era. We looked for but did not find the old family homestead - the descriptions we had been given easily fitting most of the houses we saw. I could picture Southern Belles fanning themselves in days gone by - with bourbon on the rocks or whatever other drink they plied themselves with - on the various verandas along Daphne's coast.

That being unsuccessful we backtracked to Mobile, had lunch, and drove down the western coast of the Bay. You might wonder why we did not just continue in an easterly direction since that was our ultimate goal. We were, apparently, fated.

Our objective was the causeway that connects the mainland to Dauphin Island, which in past eras was only accessible by boat.

In those days of isolation yet another of my wife's relatives (no nicknames or abbreviations assigned to date) had been the visiting doctor to the sailors that stopped by from time-to-time, or resided on the island in their retirement. I know nothing further of that part of the family history, which is probably for the best.

We drove across the causeway and visited a very nice island, a rather pleasant spot for a Gulf Coast island summer day trip. Dauphin Island might have been added to our bucket list for a future visit, but for the adventure we were about to encounter.

Logic took hold and we decided not to backtrack along the causeway. We went to the dock and waited for the ferry to arrive and take us to the eastern shore. Our own version of "Sitting on the Dock of the Bay." It was to be our first ferry trip ever.

We loaded onto the ferry and start the short trip east. All according to the plan for us to get to our destination by nightfall.

However, it should be noted that the wife and I, well before the marital bonds were put in place, had been shipwrecked in Galveston Bay when an afternoon squall came up while we were sailing with friends. Our sailboat, having a squall-induced broken centerboard and rudder, decided a shoal island adjacent to the Galveston Bay Ship Channel would be a suitable place to spend the hours until rescue came.

If you have never been evacuated to the mainland by a Coast Guard helicopter we highly recommend it. Could even be a bucket list item. All with a happy outcome, thank you very much, but also one that now made us very aware of squall lines coming towards us across any body of water.

Which was what was happening as we took the ferry east. We knew what was about to happen, as did the captain no doubt. He deserved the credit he was due – he almost made it.

Almost. The squall came directly at us, creating waves and winds and currents that were really rather exciting (At the time I was working as an oceanographer so I know about these things. Never dreamed that I would experience them up close and personal once, let alone twice. Some guys are just really lucky.). As the squall bore down on us, the ferry bore down on its goal, the dock. It should have been easy to land – the dock had two extended piers on each side flaring out to create sort of a funnel-type receptacle into which the ferry was to enter and tie up. Easy in theory anyway.

For quite a few minutes the captain did not even try. He did the ferry-boat equivalent of treading water in the middle of the bay waiting for the aforementioned waves, winds, and currents to abate.

Those of us on the ferry made an interesting group. The pedestrians had been on the deck in their summer floral shirts and shifts, looking forward to landing and whatever they had planned to do on the mainland. Half of the automotive passengers were also on deck, the other half in their cars napping or whatever.

After the rocking and rolling began, all the pedestrians disappeared – not overboard to the best of my knowledge – and the outdoor half of the automotive passengers got into their cars, probably praying or whatever was their own particular bent.

Funny how one's mind works in such moments. I can swim, I said to myself, what if we sink? Will I be the lone survivor? Make it to shore easily or with great difficulty? The momentary local hero/survivor everyone feels sorry for? An opportunity to start life anew?

No, not really. My mind never went there. Just thought I would get you started.

The captain tries landing number one. On go the ferry's afterburners and it tries to head straight for the dock. The current pushes us to the flared pier on the right however and a full retreat was ordered.

Time passes.

Landing number two. This time the flared pier on the left is in our sights. Retreat number two.

Landing number three was successful. We did not wait to see how many people kneeled and kissed the ground (though we are pretty sure the Pope was not onboard with us). Off we went as fast as our backfiring vehicle would take us.

Not far down the road we realized that the longer time than planned spent looking for the old family homestead and trying to get to the dock on the east side of the bay meant we were not going to make our destination that day. So, as night began to fall, we started looking for a suitable hotel. I did my duty at one of these establishments, asking the hotel attendant about vacancy, costs, etc., returning to the car for a confab before committing to a room for the night. The terms were acceptable and I returned, whereupon the same attendant for the first time asked the mid-forty-ish man in front of her for his AARP card.

I paused a moment, wondering if the adventures we had been through that day had aged me that much, but, not wanting to know the answer, politely answered in the negative.

The next day we get a good distance across the Florida panhandle on a fine, sunny Florida afternoon when a noise is heard from the left side of the car. Low at first, but increasing in volume with time. Now what?

BOOM. Yes, a tire blew out. We manage to follow the recommended course of action and safely get to the side of the road where we start unpacking the car to get to the spare tire.

The golf clubs came out of the trunk first, followed by the usual mandatory duet of mini-suitcases holding, respectively, jewelry and makeup, and the larger suitcase with everything else that was needed by my Southern Belle. I presume I also had a suitcase.

So there we are. All of the above stacked on the side of the road, a Southern Belle under a golf umbrella to protect her delicate complexion from the Gulf's summer sun, me on my knees trying to change the tire. The blowout was, of course, on the left side of the car, putting me just that many inches from the passing cars and trucks.

I jack the car up, and remove the lug nuts and the bad tire. All per plan.

But wait there is more. A fast moving semi-truck with a trailer in tow rumbles by at what seemed to a speed of Mach 1 at least. What one might expect on a highway.

Perhaps, but what one might *not* expect is that the change in air pressure created by that truck was just enough to cause the car to vibrate and blow the jack out from under the car – of course at just the moment when the bad tire was off but the good one not yet on, thus providing the car the opportunity to have the axle make contact with the pavement.

Holy Cow Batman!

Fortunately, all of this occurred at a moment when no hands were under the car, or on the jack, or in fact anywhere near the place where the axle contacted the pavement. Being on my knees, though,

I was able to fully experience an up close and personal perspective of the jack's departure from its intended duty.

So there we are. In the middle of who knows where, a blown-out tire, a jack not under the car, a non-blown-out tire not on the axle, a women sitting on her suitcase under an umbrella, and a set of golf clubs with no golf course in sight.

A really happy ending would be that a good guy stops by with all the tools to get the car back on the jack and we move on with our vacation.

But remember we did not win anything while gambling in Biloxi.

Somehow we did manage to get the jack back to where it was supposed to be and the spare tire where we wanted it to be. The tire was, of course, one of those you cannot drive very far or at a very high speed, so our next stop was Tallahassee (Go Seminoles!), where a suitable replacement tire was found, though not inexpensively.

By then we were not far from our ultimate destination, and were quite relieved not to have any real opportunity for further highway adventures.

Funny thing. I don't remember any other part of this vacation. We probably played golf. We might also have played miniature golf. We no doubt had some good meals. But I remember nothing.

Nothing other than the adventure from Texas to Florida in Leota Myer Hess's Chrysler Sedan.

About the Author

Steve Koch retired from ExxonMobil Corporation on Independence Day, July 4, 2015 after a career in science, engineering, and the law.

Over the course of his career, he wrote frequently, publishing in the fields of oceanography, ocean engineering, and the law. His first book, *The Thinking Golfer's Manual: What Amateurs Need to Know*, was published in 2018.

He has engineering and science degrees from Purdue University, the Massachusetts Institute of Technology, and the Woods Hole Oceanographic Institute, and a law degree from the University of Houston Law Center.

He lives outside of Houston, Texas with his wife and the manager of the household, a cat named Maximilian Bonaparte.

Duke, Me & the Men in the Sheets

By Curt Locklear

Duke, Me & the Men in the Sheets

WHAT CAN I SAY THAT I know about this vast stretch of land called Texas? Its constant battles since its beginnings with settlers fighting Comanche raiders or escaping Karankawa cannibals. Pirates prowled the coast and harbored in Galveston. Texans fought for independence from Mexico, fought in the Mexican War, in the Civil War, and in modern wars as well.

In the 1930's, vast dust storms that blanketed northern and west Texas, so you could look a long while without seeing a single plant. But the roots were there.

But our longest war has always been against a small cadre of hate-filled men. My story is about my first encounter with that sort of man.

The brief rain in the fall of 1956 didn't help much. The seven-year drought was still crushing the Texas farms and ranchlands, including our cattle lot. I had worked all day during the intermittent rain, helping my papa use the blowtorch to burn the needles off the prickly pear so that the cows would have something to eat. Such was most of my endeavors on that fateful Saturday. It was in the evening that an unexpected event transpired where lives teetered on a precipice.

My family lived on the last vestige of town, on the last street of the neighborhood before there was nothing. Oh, there was dusty, rocky land, and scrub oaks, and spiny mesquite trees in sun-scorched grass pastures, but that was about all. A few pitiful goat and sheep farms stretched along the dirt road that led out past our house to the west Texas mesas.

After an early supper, my parents left to drive to the church for a planning meeting for the Fall Bazaar.

Mama told me, "Steven, you stay in this house until we get back. Do you hear me?"

"Yes, ma'am." I didn't look up, but stared at the newspaper on the coffee table. The headline read: 1956 Looks to Be Record Driest Year."

I pushed the newspaper aside and played solitaire awhile.

In the drought, with any slight breeze, the road's dust hung like a cloud that never settled. Dust blew across our parched lawn and in our screen door. I heard the dirt scratching the screen.

Being ten-years-old, I was bored to the point of feeling paralyzed. A tube of the TV had burned out, so the TV didn't work.

I sprang from the couch, and I phoned friend after friend to see if anyone could come over and play. Ferdinand was gone to visit an aunt. Peaches had the mumps. Freddie and Eddie were just leaving with their parents for some event with relatives. Freddie did not sound happy. He intimated that another family blow-up had occurred. I hung up the phone in disgust. It was Saturday, but nothing good was showing at the Texan Theatre or at the Palace. A Bela Lugosi vampire movie at one, and a Deborah Kerr movie at the other, just a "dumb" romance. So, hoping for my parents to return home and take me to a movie was useless. I had not played all day.

In a moment of wildness, I determined to bicycle down to Duke's house and play with his kids. Duke worked for my papa, and he had, two days before, made a sworn statement to the sheriff about who he thought the men were who had done the cattle rustling on the M-Bar ranch.

His kids and I had played once before just a few days after they moved in to what all the neighbor kids and fellow cyclists called the *haunted house* on the old dirt road. It was a large, but ramshackle old domicile that sat on land that was long unused and overgrown with brush and brambles.

I reasoned that Duke and his kids would be just as happy to see me as I would be to see them. It didn't bother me at all that I, a white kid, was playing with Negroes.

I liked them, even if they went to the Dunbar all-blacks school, and they liked me.

I did not notice, or perhaps ignored, how late it was getting, and since I reasoned that I'd just be gone only a short while, and I knew that, after the church meeting, my parents were always visiting the old folks' home. I left a note on the table saying where I was should they return early.

It was turning autumn chilly, so I threw on a blue-jean jacket, scooted out the back door, jumped on my bicycle and pedaled hard down the rocky, dusty road that led out of town, but it first passed where Duke lived. The sun was setting off to my right, crimson rays spreading out like long spears at the horizon. The orange, harvest half-moon ducked in and out of a gloomy patchwork of clouds that flowed like floating islands across the sky.

No cars or trucks traversed the road this late. People were already home sitting down to supper. The road was mine.

Despite the muddiness, I glided easily down the damp hill road, weaving in great S-shaped curves over its entirety. I turned on my bicycle headlamp. Noticing the encroaching dark, I promised myself that I would only stay at Duke's house a little while. The recent rain caused a gray fog to gather over the damp road, the thickets, and fields. I reached the straightaway, and I saw the glow of Duke's house lights off to the right through the thicket. Such a big, rambling old ranch house. "I guess it's not haunted after all," I reassured myself even as the last vestiges of light wore away behind the dense brush and trees.

Somehow, the house lights seemed brighter than I expected. Many smaller beams, like beads of fairy light caught in a gossamer web, flickered through the foggy mist in their yard. I thought the sight quite pretty. I wondered what was going on at their house.

When I turned into the lengthy, black loam driveway leading to Duke's home, the house lights switched off. Murky shadows surrounded the house. I stood up, pushing hard on my pedals, for the road mud was thick. Little pools of water reflected the moonlight along the trenches and in the potholes. The day's rain had not dried yet. The earth smelled wet. It was such a rare smell in those dry years that I let it swell in my nostrils.

Churning my bicycle through the mud, I came up beside three pickups parked in the grass beside the dirt drive. Past the pickups, my headlamp illuminated a great number of deep footprints in the still moist soil. Several men had passed that way. Did Duke's family have other visitors tonight? Why had the visitors not driven up to the house? I followed the curve of the drive around to allow me a full view of the house, and then I saw something that I did not, at first, understand.

Ghosts floated in the heavy mist about the yard. Many ghosts. Gray and dull white specters hovered in the yard, passing in and out of the foggy illumination of many beams of light. Three specters stood holding torches, the flame licking the darkness, casting the ghosts sometimes into shadow, sometimes into light. I braked hard to a stop and killed my bicycle lamp.

Cold fear like tiny knives swept over my body. My breath quickened. Real ghosts passed before me a scant forty yards away. With crickets striking up their symphony, night crowded in on all sides. Somehow, I forced myself to walk the bicycle forward to peer through the gloom.

My mind slowly made more sense of the scene unfolding. I realized that the figures before me were not ghosts, but men dressed in sheets and with tapered hoods on their heads. Just as I comprehended this and regained my breath, one of the men on the porch called out, gruff and fierce.

"We know you're inside, Duke. We ain't got no issue with your family. We just want you out here."

The porch light flashed on, intense and broad, illuminating the entire yard as well. Some of the men dressed in what I considered at that moment to be Halloween dress-up garb stepped back a little, put their arms at their heads to ward off the light shining bright in their eyes.

Many voices called out in the glare and shadow - angry voices, curses and epithets.

I didn't know the meaning of their anger, nor their cause. I remembered seeing a faded picture in an old newspaper of men in sheets with pointed head dressings. I didn't know what that costume meant. As if on cue, the group of men moved as one towards the porch, slogging through the muddy yard. I counted six men - the large one on the porch, three of average build, one fat one, one small one.

All their attention focused on the house. I felt they could not see me in the blackness cast by the house and thicket. I inched my bicycle closer. I stood in the pedals and pumped hard against the muddy soil to just outside the porch lights' illumination. I sat astride my bicycle.

I did not feel brave. I felt numbed. I understood that these men meant harm to Duke. But I didn't know what to do. Did Duke's family have a telephone to call for help? Should I ride back to the road and try to flag down a passing motorist?

The large man on the porch pounded on the door, "Alright, nigger, you don't leave us no choice." The voice sounded familiar. My thoughts jumped to Stengal, the town's adult bully.

But, no, it was not his voice. I would know his voice anywhere. But the large man sounded similar, a crustiness to his words, a drawing, ambling bravado. The other men's voices were too mixed together to tell any of them.

Then the knot of men stepped onto the porch.

At that moment, I realized that they could, at any time, turn and catch sight of me and that I would be hard pressed to get away, especially on the muddy drive. I fought the urge to turn and run. The men banged on the door and windows of the house. One man hurled a rock through a window. A baby wailed loud and long inside the house. While the men banged and threatened, I saw the shadowy door at the back of the house open just a bit, then close.

I heard a woman's voice call from inside. It was a strong voice, one with no fear, but of resignation. "My husband ain't here. You're wasting your time. He ain't done nothing to you anyway."

"Well, maybe you'll tell us where we can find him."

"I don't know where he is. And besides, you done scared my baby."

"Well, ain't that too bad."

"It sure is bad, if I call the sheriff on you."

"That won't do you a bit of good to try." Several of the men chuckled.

"Well, I done called him."

"I don't think you called him, cause we cut your phone wires. Now let us in before we kick down this door."

One man drew a sledgehammer out from under his sheet. "Want me to use this now?"

The big man stepped aside to give the other man with the sledgehammer room to swing.

The big man called again, "This is your last chance."

The baby bawled, the other children called out in fear from the house. I couldn't understand what they were saying.

From inside the house, Duke's wife's voice rose above her children's wails. "Quiet, all of you. All right, I'm opening the door. You best not do anything to my children or my house."

The men stepped back. The door handle turned.

Off to my right, I heard a whispered "No!" I turned to see, about twenty paces from me, a black man in a white T-shirt. It was Duke, crouching behind a crepe myrtle bush.

"Duke!" I called in a whisper.

He looked at me. "Get down, little Steven, if they see you, they just as soon put your eyes out or kill you."

I lay my bicycle down and slipped over behind the bush beside Duke.

The door of the house opened, and Duke's wife emerged, her light cotton dress clinging to her thin frame. She stood square in the doorway, and she stretched her arms across it. "Ain't none of you going in my house unless you promise..."

"Get out the way, you black whore." The big man, pushed her arm down and swept past her, followed by the others. I saw the lights come on in the house. A plate crashed to the floor and I could hear the storm of tramping feet and furniture scraping through the house. Children's voices cried.

Out on the road, a police siren sounded. We turned to see flashing lights and two high beams churning up the road, tires spinning through the mud. The patrol car sped past our vantage point and slid to a stop right in the yard. All the sheet-clad men clambered out of the house onto the porch, one of them knocking Duke's wife onto the ground. She lay there only for a moment, then jumped up and ran past them and back into the house.

The driver's side patrol car's door swung wide. With revolver drawn, out stepped Deputy Ludlow. With his shallow chin, and weakened frame, he looked like barely a wisp of a man. He leaned his scrawny arms across the top of his car, the lights still flashing. He aimed his revolver at the cluster of men on the porch. He called out. "You men are through for tonight. Get off the porch now." His voice shook a little.

"Well, if it ain't Deputy Ludlow." The big man stepped forward from the group. "I thought you'd be up here with us helpin' us out, seein' as how..."

"Shut your trap. I mean to shoot you if you don't do as I say. Get down off the porch. Leave this family alone."

"What! You turned into a nigger lover, Ludlow?" The other men called out as well.

"Yeah, you a nigger lover?"

Ludlow turned his gun up into the air and fired. The gang of men stopped their harangue.

He aimed again at the men. "You don't know anything about me. I just know you ain't doing nothing to this family. I don't care what else you do, but you ain't gonna harm Duke, nor his family."

I turned to look at Duke. The expression on his face showed disbelief. We had both been there in the sheriff's office when Deputy Ludlow had shown an uncaring disposition when Duke made his statement about the rustling of the cattle. Duke shook his head, confused. Then, he patted me on the shoulder to let me know he was leaving. He removed his white t-shirt and slipped around in the dark to his back porch while the men still faced Deputy Ludlow.

The sheet-men on the porch would not budge. Deputy Ludlow re-aimed his gun. The small man who had hung back in the yard had disappeared from my sight. Deputy Ludlow and the sheet-covered men continued to throw words back and forth.

Directly, I made out movement on the back porch – Duke and his family slipping away into the thicket. I saw them blend into the darkness, then nothing. I sneaked out from hiding, grabbed my bicycle and pulled it behind the bush.

Deputy Ludlow stepped out from behind the car, his revolver still aimed at the men.

"Look, I know who each one of you are. And there's plenty of people, like some judges, or maybe some reporters out of Dallas, that would love to know what you're doing here..."

No sooner had he spoken than a new set of headlights appeared on the mud road. No flashing lights, but the car was churning up the road towards the house. It stopped, engine running, lights shining, a few yards back from my position. Then more cars arrived and lined up a few yards apart out on the county road, perhaps as many as ten cars. Figures, merely dark shadows, stepped out from the cars, silhouetted.

The fat sheet-man stepped forward and leaned his face to the big man's ear, cupping his hand. The big man nodded, but said nothing. He waved the others to follow him. They came down off the porch and strolled unhurried out from the house and into the muddy field towards their pickups. They passed within a few feet of me. They were swearing under their breath.

As they drew even to my hiding place, the fat man turned his head towards me. I saw his eyes, and he seemed to be looking straight at me, but he never broke stride. After a few paces, he turned his head forward again.

They passed the parked car, the engine running, the headlights glaring. I could not see who drove it. It was so dark, I could just make out the five men climbing into their own pickups, turning on the headlights, and starting up the engines. I do not know where the sixth man went.

All three pickups backed up the driveway, the wheels spinning in the mud, onto the county road, and drove away past the other parked cars.

I heard one of the men call, "We'll be back, nigger."

Deputy Ludlow holstered his pistol, got into his car, backed up, turned the vehicle, and drove past me. As far as I could tell, he never saw me. The other car turned around and left as well, followed by the cars out on the county road.

I gazed into the darkness that now pervaded the house and grounds. I called Duke's name many times, but he did not answer. Either he was far away in the thicket out of earshot, or too frightened for the welfare of his family to come out of hiding. Soon, I could not see the hand in front of my face, the moon behind a dark cloud. I got on my bike, flicked on the headlamp, and pedaled home. I felt weary beyond telling.

When I finally arrived back home, my papa was still gone, but my mama was there. After my mama finished her admonitions about being worried sick about me, I told her about what had transpired. She asked me many questions, then after I had told as much as I could remember, she told me to sit on the couch and wait for Papa. I did what I was told.

When Papa arrived, I heard Mama meet him at the back door and fill him in to the shortened version of the event. He came and sat beside me. "So, you had a little adventure tonight." His first comment seemed flippant. I knew he was trying to put me at ease that I was not in trouble. Then his tone changed. "Steven, is what your mother told me true?"

I looked up at Mama who stood behind him. "Yes, sir."

"And did you see the men in the white sheets break into Duke's house?"

"Yes, sir."

"Was anybody hurt?"

"I don't think so."

"Very well. I have my work cut out for Duke and his family. I've got to go see to their safety now. But first, are you all right, Steven? Are you frightened?"

I thought about the question. I felt nothing. No fear, no anxiety, just nothing. "No, Dad, I don't know why, but I'm not scared. Duke was scared. I don't know if his wife was scared. She sounded mostly mad."

My papa looked at my mama, and a quiet message passed between them, their eyes saying much.

"All right, then, Steven." Papa stood. "Irene, I have to go check on Duke. He'll have to get out of town tonight."

"Dean, be careful." Mama hugged him.

I stood and hugged him, too. The three of us stood huddled together for some time.

While I was taking a bath and later talking with my mama when she tucked me in, my papa was working to save Duke. Before he left, he made one telephone call to his friend, Bill White Eagle.

He told me later that ten minutes after he knocked on Duke's front door, he was joined by Bill White Eagle who brought a van and plenty of help from the farmers and from townsfolk. After they called for many minutes and Bill honked the van's horn, Duke and his family emerged from the thicket.

While I slept, Bill White Eagle, Papa, and their friends loaded up all of Duke's family possessions and drove the family to Duke's cousins' home in the next county.

Just when the sun was peeking through the blinds in the morning, I awoke to a nightmare of ghosts with bloody knives and gouged out eyes. I sat up, breathing hard. Finally, my head cleared. I realized I was in my own bed and sunk into the warm security of the sheets. I buried my head in the pillow and cried a little. I was not sure if I was crying for Duke and his family or for me.

I heard a soft shuffle.

I opened one eye and looked out from the pillow into my room, lit only a little by the rising sun. I saw Papa's pants legs, stained with mud. He stood by the bed. My angle afforded me no better view. Papa spoke softly, his tone sorrowful. "Steven, Duke and his family are safe. I thought you'd like to know."

"Okay," I mumbled into the pillow.

He left, and I stayed there, thinking a long time.

About the Author

Curt Locklear is a native born Texan, having grown up in Brady, Texas, which is the "Heart of Texas," being that it is at the geographical center of Texas. Can't get more Texan than that. He also grew up in Austin and attended Austin schools and the University of Texas.

He helped his father at the Brady thoroughbred horse stables and assisted in the Jockey room while the jockeys prepared for the races. He has herded cattle and sheep, hot walked horses, and mucked out their stalls, and stretched barbwire fence.

He has three children of whom he is very proud and who are all teachers, like their father. The winner of a Short Story Literary Journal Contest -first place, he also has two second place finishes, a third place and an honorable mention. So much for small awards.

He has two published novels, mostly 5 Star rated. Even New York Times best-selling author, Robert Hicks, praised the first book, *Asunder*. Every professional reviewer gave *Splintered* 5 Stars. An avid guitar and banjo player, his banjo playing is featured on the hit PBS series, "The Daytripper with Chet Garner." A retired educator, Mr. Locklear has taught English, History and Journalism. He even composed the Alma Mater school songs for four schools.

He expresses his gratitude and is indebted to a great number of wonderful supporters and many dear friends and am a proud member of Houston Writers House. He is blessed.

Connect with Curt on Facebook
E-mail: curt@curtlocklearauthor.com

Ghosts of Chinese New Year
By F.S. Lynch

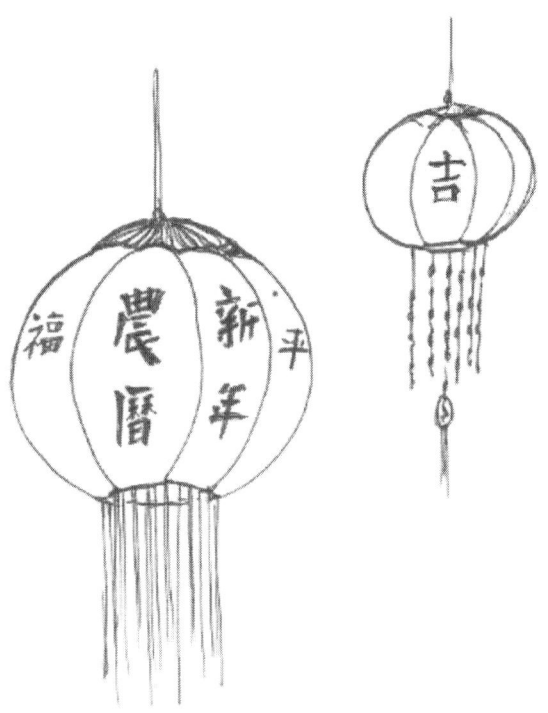

Ghosts of Chinese New Year

AS SOON AS THE CUSTOMER walked in, Lina knew he was trouble. The man's white Armani suit and slicked back hair contrasted with the paper parasols and lucky Chinese symbols on the wall. Outside the shop, the neon sign of Emperor Ming's Chinese Emporium bathed the front window in blue light. The Emporium was a tourist dive in one of Houston's busiest China Town plazas. People dressed in two thousand-dollar suits did not stroll into the shop unless they were looking for something unscrupulous.

Lina rubbed a hand across her eyes. This should have been an easy day at the shop. In fifteen minutes, Ma would close early for Chinese New Year. Lina popped out her earbud and set down her cell phone with a thud on the glass case. Inside the cabinet, fake jade jewelry and tiny lacquered boxes rattled at her carelessness. Lina clucked her tongue. *Worthless baubles.* Ma kept the expensive and dangerous stuff in the back. The jewelry was only there to deter any would be "bank robbers" as *Wai Po*, Lina's grandma, called them.

In her most obnoxious voice, Lina yelled, "*Ma, Ke Lan!*" Mom, Customer. There had only been a trickle of customers coming into the shop since Ma decided to open at the crack of dawn. For Lina, dawn meant nine AM. Why on all days did a customer choose to come in on Chinese New Year? More importantly, on the eve of her one year dating anniversary with Winston?

Lina anticipated this day all month long. She had promised to be her Ma's slave for the rest of her miserable life, if she could have the night off. Usually, Chinese New Year was a week-long celebration reserved for spending time with family and forgetting the misfortunes of the year past. Stuffing yourself with black sesame rice balls, slippery fish, and meat and leek dumplings until you burst was an added bonus.

"Can I help you?" Lina asked, as the customer ducked his head under a row of paper lanterns.

Lina eyed the customer. The man looked like he was Italian with his wavy black hair tied in a ponytail, dark skin and lint-free suit. His black silk tie swarmed around his neck like an eel.

"Yes, I'm looking for Mistress Ching. You look a little young to be her." The man said, his eyes roamed down the golden buttons of Lina's tight lilac *chi-pao* shirt that Ma forced her to wear "to appear Chinese." In open rebellion, Lina had paired it with jeans with more holes than Swiss cheese.

"That's my Ma," Lina cleared her throat. "Is there something specific you wanted? We have a one of a kind porcelain tea set made by a famous artist in Taiwan." That was a lie. They were manufactured in a dumpy factory in China, but Lina didn't care as long as the man bought something and left.

Didn't Ma hear me shout? What's taking so long?

The customer smiled. "My boss is interested in more insubstantial things." The man stepped closer. Lina could smell his expensive Clive Christian cologne.

In a low voice he whispered, "I hear this is where I can buy *gui?*"

Lina's smile dropped. All the pretty bowls and jade dragons were really a front for the Emporium's true business: dealing in captured Chinese demons and ghosts. Ma handled those type of customers directly. The knot in her stomach unclenched at the sound of the tinkle of beads from behind.

"*Fan Ying Guan Ling,*" Ma said, her brown eyes angry as she glanced at Lena.

They seemed to say *why didn't you call me sooner?* Ma Ching was dressed in a cream-colored chi-pao embroidered with golden flowers. Her hair shone unnaturally black, thanks to the hair dye she used liberally. But Ma's face was still beautiful, with her un-wrinkled skin and red painted lips.

"I'm Su Ching, owner of this Emporium."

"My name is Armando. I would like to see some of the wares you have in the back."

"He's looking for *gui.*" Lina dropped the words like hot coals.

Ma shot Lina a look that could burn through silk. Lina folded her arms across her chest. *What? I was trying to be helpful.*

"Of course," Ma simpered. "But we always ask for payment up front and no returns."

The man withdrew several items from the pocket of his suit. He laid on Ma's outstretched hand three ancient gold coins and a folded piece of white paper. Lina could see the strokes of the Chinese characters through the translucent note.

Ma put on her jeweler's glasses. Her brown eyes appeared owlish as she studied the coins.

With a nod, Ma said, "Come with me."

When Armando pushed his way through the strings of beads that covered the back door, Lina let out a sigh. *Good riddance.* She didn't need customers like that fifteen minutes from closing. She walked back to the counter and texted Winston on her phone.

Can't wait to see you tonight!

Lina looked at the mirror and adjusted the lace collar of her scarlet dress that had a v-neckline that plunged past her breasts. She pulled on black leggings. Winston's eyes were going to pop. The door to her room creaked open which forced Lina to pluck the black leather jacket from the back of her chair. Hastily, she zipped up the front.

"Don't think you can fool me, *Lanying*. You're going to see that *bai gui*, aren't you?" an old voice like crinkled paper croaked.

Lina turned around to see her *Wai Pao* in the doorway. Her grandma wore her steely-white hair in a bun and had on a red-bean colored vest with long sleeves. Her strong arms clinked with jade bracelets and a carved golden Buddha hung down her thick neck.

"Wai po," Lina whined, "Please don't call Winston the white demon. That is so rude!"

"Why?" Wai Po muttered. "That's what he is, a white demon. We come from a line of demon hunters a thousand years old.

We are a proud family, why should my granddaughter marry a foreigner! You'll marry someone of your rank. A prominent demon hunter from the Tang or Sun clan."

Lina's eyebrows shot up. "I'm seventeen years old! Why would any of the prominent clans even want me, a demon hunter born with no magic? You've met Winston dozens of times. He's sweet and respectful of our culture." Lina's heart sank. She hated reminding Wai Po of Ma's failure to produce offspring with demon blood. She had to get Wai Po off her back.

Wai Po huffed, showing her yellowed teeth gleaming with gold crowns. Her eyes softened at the mention of Lina's disability. One wrinkled hand reached for her granddaughter's arm.

"That *bai gui* has bewitched you. Now hurry downstairs, your Ma wants to see you."

Lina pulled her leather jacket tighter and slipped by her Wai Po's disapproving glare. She breathed a sigh of relief. Thank Heaven and Earth for her Wai Po's bad eyes. As she crept down the stairs of their townhome barefoot, Lina ran through the excuses she had prepared if Ma asked her to unzip her jacket. *Ma it's our one-year anniversary, I just wanted to look nice. Ma, all the other girls at school wear sluttier clothes. Ma I have my chicken sickles, I'll cut off his hand if he lays a finger on me.* Lina scoffed. She'd never lay a blade on Winston but Ma wouldn't expect less.

The entrance hall of their townhome was decorated with imported rugs and fake flowers draped on Greek columns. Her Ma waited for her dressed in a sweater and slacks. A purple bag dangled from her hand.

"I'm leaving." Lina stood on her tip toes and planted a kiss on her ma's cheek.

Ma's eyes flicked to hers. Lina took a breath and a nervous tremor shot up her spine. *Has she noticed the length of my dress?*

"Lina," Ma said putting a smile on her face, the same one she used to flatter important customers. She held out her hands, the bag dangling like some sort of dead animal. "I need you to make a delivery."

"No." The words rushed out of Lina faster than her brain could react. *No!* She had waited a month for this date.

Ma can't do this to me. Winston will be disappointed if I can't make it. Lina had always been dutiful. While other teenagers at the high school played in band or danced in short skirts in cheer, Lina was stuck behind the counter selling demons to shady customers.

"But you promised I could have the night off!" Lina's whine trickled like water out of a clogged faucet.

Ma's voice became sterner. "Be reasonable. It's the customer that came in this afternoon. He wants a rush delivery tonight in River Oaks."

"But Ma! Didn't you tell him it's Chinese New Year! The streets in Chinatown will be a nightmare!"

Ma thrust the bag into Lina's arms. "It's on your way to the restaurant you're meeting Winston at, isn't it? Just a little detour. Your motorcycle will bypass all the traffic, my little heart-liver."

Bloody Ghosts! Ma was bringing out the gross body endearments. Lina sighed.

Heart-liver, two organs a person couldn't live without. Ma hadn't called her that since she was five. She must be desperate or the customer had paid her a crap load of money for rush delivery.

"Drop off the bag and be on your way." Ma said. "It's a very important customer and I won't even say a word about that dress you're wearing or what time you should be home."

Lina tugged the skirt of her lace dress down farther. It barely reached past her thigh.

"Fine," Lina pouted.

"You have your goggles and your chicken sickles? I texted the address to you already." Ma called after her.

So that was what the chime had been. Sneaky Demon Hunter. Lina waved a hand in response and opened the front door. Her motorcycle sat in the small gated area outside. She opened the side bag, and inside lay the chicken sickles, three thin blades that looked like chicken feet, in their little compartment. Lina tucked the box on top of her weapons and buckled on her helmet. She hopped on the motorcycle, pulled the choke, and turned her key in the ignition. With a squeeze of the clutch and a press of the start button, the motorcycle shuddered to life. As she sped off into the traffic, Lina's mind raced. Her date with Winston, at a trendy restaurant in Midtown, was a good forty minutes away. Lina had given herself an hour to get there and now she had to make a stop in River Oaks.

At a stoplight, stuck behind a long line of cars, Lina texted Winston. "*Will be late. Ma forced me to make a delivery. Sorry.*"

To her right, the blare of traditional Chinese music reverberated. She could just make out the furry crimson and gold body of the dragon as it wormed its way through the crowd gathered outside the Chinese supermarket. The dragon dance hid four dancers who performed acrobatics and harassed the small children for fun. With a ping of sadness, Lina felt a bit of regret for missing the festivities.

The light turned green and Lina rushed off into the fray. *Bloody Ghosts.* She'd forgotten to ask Ma what kind of demons were in the box. Not that it mattered. Ma's seals were legendary. The little yellow and green twisted strands of thread over the box's lid were almost unbreakable.

Lina hadn't seen Winston in weeks since he been on family vacation in Belize. Winston would drive straight from the airport to their date. He had even asked Lina to come with his family on vacation. But Ma had made a hard rule: no overnight trips with the boyfriend even with his family in the same hotel. If this delivery spoiled her date, she would find that customer and release some *Huli Jing,* fox demons, into his house.

The GPS told her to make a right turn onto a backstreet to avoid traffic. Lina turned onto a two-way lane overgrown with grass and littered with abandoned buildings. Her mind was still preoccupied with Winston's kissable lips, when a car's headlights blinded her.

Lina beeped her horn, but the car kept coming. Lina pushed down on the horn harder. *Doesn't he see me?*

A scream ripped through her throat as she veered off over the side of the pavement and straight into a ditch. The black Mercedes rushed by without stopping. Lina's heart pounded. *Bloody ghosts!* Her bike slid into the ditch and her right-side scraped along the filth as she came to a halt. Thank the Heavens and Earth she had sense enough to wear her leggings underneath her dress.

Luckily, the miniature wings she had installed on her motorcycle had kicked in just in time to slow her fall. A gift from a bird *gui* her mother had coerced into a favor. Lina lay sideways letting the pounding of her heart slow. She wrenched her arm out from the sewage and crawled out from under her bike.

She took off her helmet and shrugged off her jacket to look at her arm. Pain sizzled down her skin. Some cuts and bruises but nothing hurt enough to be broken. Thanks to her Ma's persistence that she train her body like a warrior, the fall could have been worse.

Lina righted her motorcycle and opened the side bag. *Empty.* Lina's heart beat a staccato in her chest, her throat suddenly as dry as her Wai Po's skin.

Where is the box?

She spotted the box lying on its side near the storm drain. Lina bent down and clutched the box to her chest. She ran a finger across the seal. Still in-tact. The lid of the box was slightly warped and a crack had formed between the lid of the box and the base.

Had Ma failed to seal it properly?

Lina knew better than to open the box and look. Instead she hurried back up to her motorbike.

From her side bag, she pulled out a pair of blue goggles with wrap around panes. Lina may be a useless demon hunter with no powers, but she made up for it in technology.

The googles were her own invention and allowed her to see the demons that her Ma and Wai Po could see naturally with their eyes. Linda adjusted the dials on the goggles and turned in a circle. Above her, a small ripple shot across the sky. Lina ran toward it, her boots squelching in the mud, as she turned the dials on her goggles to slow down the demon's speed.

Thank the Heavens and Earth! Only one *gui* had escaped. The taunting *gui* hovered in front of Lina, a sliver of a tongue shot out at her. The *gui* was a female with iridescent blue scales that shimmered down her cheeks and across her bare breasts. The *gui's* legs ended in a fish tail. *Shui gui,* water demon. The spirit of a drown person who pulled the living down into the murky depths of any body of water and possessed their bodies. The *shui gui* sped off as soon as it saw Lina starting at it.

Lina hipped back onto her motorbike. She eased it up the incline and back onto the road. The *shui gui* would be drawn to the closest body of water. If Lina didn't catch it before the *gui* hurt someone, she would never forgive herself.

Her cell phone rang.

Lina ignored it. Five minutes later at a traffic jam, the phone rang again. When she saw Winston's name on the screen, her heart leapt a beat.

He won't be upset I'm late, will he?

"Lina, are you ok?" Winston asked.

"I'm fine. I'm sorry, I-"

"You don't sound fine. You sound out of breath. What's wrong?"

Lina bit back her anger. Her mother was going to kill her and Winston was going to dump her. She took a deep breath and told him everything that happened. Winston knew all her secrets and still stayed with her. It was part of the reason why she loved him.

"Where do you think its going?" he asked.

"To the closest body of water. Hermann Park, maybe?"

"I'll be there in fifteen minutes to help."

"You can't do any-"She heard a click and the call ended.

Lina slammed a hand against the dashboard. Now she'd gotten Winston involved.

When she arrived at Hermann Park, the fountains were going off in brilliant arcs of water. Cobblestones lined each side of the reflection pool and glowing lanterns illuminated the families and lovers walking down the park's many pathways. Children chased each other as parents watched with careful eyes.

Lina worked her way through the crowds. She turned in circles, waiting to catch the shimmer of the *gui's* aura.

"Lina," someone called.

She spotted Winston's tall skinny frame. His cheeks were red from running and his honey blond hair tousled. He was dressed in an orange plaid button down shirt and khakis, a change from his usual jeans and t-shirt look. Totally normal American boy except he was wearing knee high wader boots, a large brimmed fisherman's hat and had a net slung across one shoulder.

"What are you wearing?" Lina snorted.

Winston hugged her, a mischievous grin on his face. "What, don't I look hot? It's my demon-catching gear."

Lina shoved a finger into his chest and dug out her spare goggles. "Here. You look ridiculous. These will be more helpful. The *gui* will be a shimmer. Like a nasty pixie with a lot of teeth." Winston nodded and ran off.

With her goggles on the entire scene was bathed in a blue light. An empty stage lay at the end of the reflection pool. Off to the side, a row of hedges led to the Japanese tea gardens. She scanned the water looking for the *gui*. A child screamed a short distance away and Lina's heart raced. She zoomed in with her goggles.

The child screamed again as her brother splashed water on her from the reflection pool. People stared as Lina ran haphazardly in circles with her arms outstretched.

"It's new VR game!" she explained to one man who asked. "It's called Ghost Hunt. Everyone's playing it."

Exactly. I'm going to catch invisible creatures only I can see. The joke's on me. After her third time around the pool. Lina wondered if her intuition had been wrong. Maybe the *gui* found some other water source. Lina collapsed onto the damp grass. She could deliver the box to the client without the *gui*. She could explain that she had an accident or that her mother had miscounted the demons. An image of her Ma's disapproving eyes and a tight frown on her lips haunted Lina's mind.

Goodbye motorbike privileges. Goodbye phone. Goodbye Winston.

Winston rushed up to her grinning like he had won the lottery. The net bounced on his shoulder as he moved.

"I got it!" he yelled, causing people to turn their heads. He ducked his head sheepishly and skidded to a stop. There was a shimmer in the net and Lina's heart suddenly lightened.

*Winston the reliable! Winston the magnificent-*Lina stopped her praises for him mid-sentence. The *gui* in the bag looked much bigger than she remembered. When she went to inspect it, the *gui* appeared in a white Chinese robe with streaming black hair covered her face.

"Heavens and Earth!" Lina shouted. "That's a wild *nu gui*-put it back! Now!"

Winston's smile dropped. The ghost woman moaned and shook the net violently.

"But you told me it would be a shimmer."

"A small shimmer!" Lina yelled. "We can't fight such a large ghost."

Lina tore the seals from the fishing net and *nu gui* pulled Winston a good three feet until he had the sense to let go. The *nu gui* flew out with a horrible shriek. Her black hair was like smoke in the night air. Lina held her breath, hoping the ghost wouldn't take revenge. She ignored the hurt on Winston's face as she watched the *nu gui's* movements.

The *nu gui* shouted, "Get that *shui gui* out of my territory!" The white robes fluttered across the sky until it went over the hedge to the tea garden.

Lina grabbed Winston's hand, but he hesitated.

"Do you want me to stay back?" he asked.

Lina looked up into his blue eyes. They had lost the playfulness from moments ago. An apology stuck in her throat, but she didn't say anything.

"There's more seals in my bag. Just watch my back."

Lina's stepped carefully across the bridge that crossed over the small pond filled with koi. Her heart beat a staccato. This was her last chance. The *shui gui* stooped on a rock near the edge, gleefully spraying passerby's with water. Lina threw the seal around the *shui gui*'s neck but it darted away. She managed to grab the *gui's* tail with one fist. The shui gui dragged Lina into the pond through moss, rocks and startled fish. Lina choked as she spat dirty pond water out.

It wasn't until Winston grabbed her by the legs that she was able to wrench another seal out of her pocket and bind the *gui's* legs.

"Please," the *shui gui* begged in Mandarin. "Don't put me back in the box. It's dark in there and no water. I'll behave if you let me go."

With hair that was dripping wet and falling into her eyes, Lina let out a bitter laugh. "I don't bargain with demons."

She stuffed the *shui gui* into her bag and dropped the lacquered box on top, squishing it. Let the customer figure out how to get the little stinker back inside. Winston stood off to the side. He had taken off his waders and put the net in the trunk.

In a soft voice he asked, "Do you want a ride? You can leave your motorcycle here and we can pick it up later."

Lina looked down at her boots. She had treated him awfully when he was just trying to help. Exhaustion settled into her shoulders.

"Thanks, but I'll drive there."

Winston took her hand. "I'll follow you to make sure you're safe."

The motorbike sputtered down the street of extravagant mansions. One house she passed had a topiary carved in the shape of a dancing elephant. When Lina's phone announced she had arrived at her destination, a knot loosened in her chest. The night was almost over. She wound her way up the stone pathway, past the abundance of fairy lights and around the manicured grass. Standing in front of the 8-foot-tall mahogany door, Lina poised one finger on the doorbell. She glanced back at Winston who had parked the car on the curb, the lights still on.

Before she could even ring it, a voice came through a speaker. "No soliciting. We already have everything we want."

Lina gritted her teeth. Of course she looked like trash, what with mud staining half her dress and helmet hair that stuck up like she'd put her finger in a light socket.

"I have a delivery from Emperor's Ming's Emporium."

The door opened spilling light onto the dark pathway. A maid dressed in a frilly black and white French outfit sneered as she opened the door. Lina pasted a smile on her face like her Ma had taught her. She was tempted to hand the maid her bag including the loose *shui gui*.

"The mistress wishes to see you in person."

"I really don't have..."

"The mistress insists," the maid said.

The mansion was even more impressive on the inside. A chandelier with hundreds of crystals as big as Lina's fist hung like a jeweled necklace in the foyer. Marble with veins of gold and rose lined the hallway. Scrolls of cranes and lotus flowers hung on the walls like banners leading into a castle. Lina couldn't help but stare open-mouthed. She was painfully aware that her boots were tracking mud all over the pristine tile.

The maid led Lina into a small waiting room with two plush chairs. Lina dropped the box on the white carpet. From a wooden door at the far end emerged an elegant woman wearing a champagne colored dress and a white fox stole. The woman reminded Lina of one of the 1920's movies stars with her short curled black hair and ruby lips.

The client smiled. Her voice was soft and refined as she said in Mandarin, "Thank you for coming all this way. I know it is Chinese New Year. I apologize for taking you away from your family."

Lina stated down at the rug. "I'm sorry I'm a little late. I had some trouble on the road."

"No matter. You're here now."

The client picked up Lina's bag and lifted out the box.

"Wait," Lina cried.

A gust of wind exploded from the bag knocking the client onto her butt. Lina fumbled for the goggles she had stuffed in her jacket pocket. Expensive vases crashed to the floor and the client's face twisted in surprise. The drapes around the high windows crashed down and little dents appeared in the perfectly painted blue and gold wall. The *gui* wasn't as powerful since it wasn't close to water, but it would be all hell trying to catch it.

Winston. Winston. Winston. Lina chanted the mantra as if it would help her.

A gloved hand landed on her shoulder. Next to her, the client hissed, "What is it?"

Lina swallowed. "A *shui gui!* I got into an accident on my way here and the seal got knocked loose. I promise I'll-"

But the client wasn't listening. She was staring at the *gui*. A strange chant came from the client's lips. The *gui* suddenly stopped its movements. It flailed its arms, baring sharp teeth. Its claws dug into the last set of remaining curtains ripping the fabric to shreds.

"Come here," the client demanded, her eyes glowing like a fire had been lit within.

Lina held her breath. The curtains crashed to the floor. The *gui* clutched the flowery Persian rug. Its tiny legs pumped in the air as it resisted the call of the client.

"I said COME!" the client demanded. The command was amplified into a thousand howling cries. Lina covered her ears. Shimmering claws clutched the *gui* and dragged it to the client's feet. The *gui* cowered. Tiny hands covered its head, pupils dilated.

"Put a few more seals on it, dear." The client said in her normal voice.

Lina obeyed. She wrapped the loose bag over the *gui* and tied it with triple knots.

"Well," the client smoothed back a length of hair that had fallen into her face. "I can't excuse *gui's* for being naughty. It's in their nature."

Lina swallowed. If this got back to her Ma, she would be shut into the shop until she turned into a decrepit thirty year old. The client turned to her, took the bag from her sweating hands, and replaced it with a red envelope.

"Just call it a little tip for making a delivery on a holiday and also to replace the use of your bag," the client said.

"Th-thank you," Lina replied, dumbstruck.

She hurried out.

Outside in the walkway, Lina pried open the seal on the envelope. Five crisp one hundred-dollar bills peeked out from little golden corners. It was a tradition on Chinese New Year for elders to give children red envelopes filled with spending money. Lina tucked the envelope into her leather jacket.

Out on the street, Winston leaned on his car hood. Lina glanced at the time. It was almost ten. The night was ruined. Their reservations at the restaurant long gone. She hung her head as she approached her boyfriend.

Winston smiled. "Everything go ok with your client?"

"Not really. But I delivered the *gui*." She took a breath and put her hand on his arm. "I'm sorry for ruining our night. I understand if you don't want to see me anymore."

"Why? What are you sorry for?" Winston said, a crease appearing between his eyebrows.

"For ruining our anniversary. For dragging you through the park. For getting you involved in my crazy family's ghost hunting business."

Lina hiccupped once waiting for Winston to yell at her or worse, confirm he wanted to dump her. Instead, Winston leaned down and kissed Lina. She parted her lips in surprise. He wiped a tear from her eye. "You didn't ruin anything, *bao bao*."

Lina chuckled. Winston had confused the Chinese words for baby and babe again. "I was happy to help you. And I don't care if we eat some fancy restaurant. All I wanted to do tonight was be with the most beautiful and smartest girl I know. Whether it's wading through water, chasing *gui* or waiting for you to finish your delivery."

"Really?"

"Yes," Winston said, grinning. "Most memorable first date anniversary I've had. I bet our favorite dumpling place is still open in China Town."

He wrapped an arm around her and Lina grinned. The gloom she had felt moments ago disappeared.

"You are the best boyfriend a girl could ask for," she shouted.

"Correction-the hottest ghost-hunting boyfriend on the planet."

Lina laughed savoring Winston's warm hand on her back. She no longer cared about being run off the road, her torn dress or the mud that clotted her hair.

For tonight, any *guis* she came across would be someone else's problem.

Maybe her luck on Chinese New Year hadn't been so bad after all.

About the Author

F.S. Lynch resides in Houston, Texas with her husband, son and two needy cats. She has a degree in supply chain management, an MBA and works for an energy firm by day. She is a member of the Houston Writers House. Her favorite genres to write in are young adult fantasy, science fiction and historical fiction. While not writing, she collects anime figures, creates miniature clay sculptures and occasionally travels the world.

Gunfight of the Century

By Stan Marshall

Gunfight of the Century

I WAS BORN RIGHT HERE in, Polecat, Texas. Well, Polecat's not its real name, just what most folks call it. The map name is Polk Flat, and Mayor Leadsman scolds anyone who calls it
Polecat. 'Course most folks don't give a coyote's howl what the mayor wants. Ordinary God-fearing townsfolk consider Mayor Leadsman to be a first cousin to the anti-Christ anyway.

In the summer of '79, I was sitting in the porch-shade of the newspaper office when Mr. Klugmann, the fella I work for two days a week, came running up the street like a wildcat was on his tail. "Lou! You're not going to believe what I just heard."

Unlikely, seeing's how just about anything seemed possible after the goings on of the past twelve years.

Eight years ago, Harry Leadsman, the bookkeeper at Jagger's Lumber Mill, was caught stealing sixty dollars from Daws Jagger's cash box. Once that word was out, Pavel Popovich, at the Red Wolf Saloon, reckoned it was Leadsman who had been stealing from him while working part-time keeping the bar Saturday nights.

By nightfall, ole Harry Leadsman was stripped down to his britches and boots, and thrown onto the evening northbound stage. They say it was one knee-slapping sight, him fencepost thin, hook nose and tiny mustache, squealing like a newborn piglet. They bought his ticket with the money on his person and divided what piddly belongings he had in his room at the boarding house between Mr. Jagger and Mr. Popovich.

To everyone's astonishment, four years later, Harry Leadsman sashayed back into town riding in a four-horse carriage with a driver and two coachmen. He sported a belly and a couple of extra chins, but it was him alright. Wearing a braid trimmed coat, gray

striped trousers, and pointy black shoes, he stepped onto the street like he was the King of Siam. He cocked his
English riding hat forward against the hot summer breeze, and footed it straight to Mr. Glum's Texas Bank and Title.

From then on, Harry Leadsman strutted around town as cocksure as you please, waiving hundred dollar banknotes around like they were nickels. By week's end, he'd bought the Hodge Hotel and the abandoned hitch and harness building next door.

Before you knew it, he'd turned the two buildings into the Palace Hotel, Saloon and Gambling House, a glorious sight to see. Chandeliers from Ireland, marble bar tops from Italy and fancy chairs from France. I'd never seen such splendor in all my nineteen years. Somehow, two months later, the town council appointed Leadsman Polk Flat's first mayor. So, no. Tain't likely I'd be surprised.

"Mayor Leadsman and Rawls Glum over at the bank are going to put on a gunning contest right here in Polk Flat."

"How do you *put on* a gunning contest?"

"They're going to put Waco Kincaid up against Gilliam Taylor in a gunfight right here on Main Street." He laughed with glee as he bowed his head and shook it. "Going to be a top hat howdy-do with a $5000 prize to the survivor."

"Survivor? You mean a sure-enough shoot and kill contest?"

"None other."

Okay, he'd done it. I was as surprised as a black bear stepping on a snap trap.

Now, the reason Mr. Klugmann was so darn googly about such an event was because he owns the Valley Weekly Notice, the only newspaper within ninety miles. With real news being as rare as rabbit wings in these parts, a shoot'em dead gunfight on Polecat's main street was a guaranteed newspaper goldmine.

Klugmann said," When the mayor and Mr. Glum heard Waco Kincaid was back in town, not two weeks after Gilliam Taylor gunned down Apache Joe Littlehorn behind Mo Fedder's Livery, they hatched up the idea of a gunfight right between the two."

"What did Sheriff Maxey say about that?"

"He didn't cotton to it much, but with the mayor and city council making all the city ordinances, there wasn't much he could do."

I asked, "How does a gunfight make Leadsman and Glum any money? Those two don't sweat a drop without cash money being in it."

"It's a humdinger of an idea." Said Klugmann." Once word gets out, people will flock into town like jackrabbits to a bean patch."

"I still don't see the profit for 'em."

"Those people will bring money. They'll need rooms, meals, shaves, baths, and beers. They'll be buying everything from pennants and ribbons to parasols and tents. Everybody's gonna make money."

I was an everybody, but didn't see anything for me, and I told him so.

"You'll make out too, "he said. "You can be my story man. I need you to tell me what Gilliam Taylor and Waco Kincaid do every minute up until the shooting-what they eat, who they talk to and where they go. People will want to know. We'll print a paper every day until the big event."

"I still...,"my voice trailed off.

As I left, I heard Mr. Klugmann mumble something about Gilliam needing a meaner sounding name like Killer or Deadshot.

I did as the boss asked but neither gunman was in a talking mood, especially Waco. His hard eyes and dark stare froze the blood right in my veins.

When I told Mr. Klugmann, he laughed. "Don't worry about it. I'll just make something up and say we got it from a drummer who passed through."

That was what Klugmann called swelling a story. "Nobody wants to read a story with nothing but true facts in it. It's up to us journalists to make the story worth their nickel."

"Fifteen cents," I corrected. Seemed a bit dishonest to me, but he claimed all newspapers did it.

For three weeks straight, Polecat was all a scamper with enterprise. The gunfight was all anybody talked about. The town council formed The Polk Flat Merchants Association, and every business in town was levied a tax for Commerce Progress and Enrichment. Every penny collected went straight to the Gunfight of the Century Event.

One Thursday morning, I was sitting on the bench under the oak next door to the newspaper building when Callie Warden scurried up. "I got some news for Mr. Klugmann. Excitin' newspaper news."

I was glad to see her, news or not. Callie and I hadn't exchanged any more than Good days, and Good afternoons the whole four years I'd known her. There were plenty of times I wanted to say more, but always got tangle-tongued.

She was clearly the prettiest girl I'd ever seen in my whole life.

"Uh, hello Miss Warden. Pleasant day, isn't it?"

"Lou Butler, I just said I had some exciting newspaper news, and all you can say is, "Hello and Pleasant day?"

"I'm, uh, sorry. What's the news?"

"Well, Maddie Fielder told me that Dorothia Glum said her pa and the mayor got Waco and Gilliam to agree to a gunfight."

Callie's deep blue eyes shined as she talked, and the sunlight framed her corn-yellow hair like a halo.

I didn't tell her she was a mite late with her gossip. Mr. Klugmann and I'd spent the day before and half the night laying out those very facts on the lettering trays? According to the story, the Mayor paid the two gunmen a hundred dollars apiece for their handshakes on the matter.

Instead, I said, "Thank you, Miss Warden. I'll tell Mr. Klugmann."

She gave me a heart-stopping smile and swirled around to go, her gingham skirt twirling in the morning breeze.

"I was wondering…" A buckboard rumbled and swallowed up my words as Callie glided back down the street. I wanted to ask her to the Independence Dance, but like every time before, my tongue and mind refused to agree.

I usually delivered lumber for Jagger's Lumber Mill on Thursdays and Fridays, but the mill sawed boards for the grandstands all week.

They didn't need a wagoneer to haul the boards fifty feet up the street, so I sallied back to Ruby Maldacci's, where I roomed, to see if she had extra work for me.

She didn't but asked me if I could stay at the newspaper or lumber mill for the week of the gunfight.

"I'll give you free boarding for the rest of the month." She'd already had inquiries to rent her three empty rooms and four cots in the parlor for Gunfight Week—all at double price."

I agreed. Ruby'd been like a grandma to me ever since my folks died of the fever three years back. I worked Wednesdays for her, muckin' her stable, and fixin' things around the place and she gave me half price rent. Ruby's wasn't much, but it was all *I* could afford.

As I returned to the newspaper office, a blatant string of vulgar cussing from across the street burned up my ears. There on the front walk of the Palace Hotel, Saloon and Gambling House, our esteemed mayor was having himself a hissy-fit to beat all hissy-fits. Daniel, his poor mop boy, cringed and cowed against the wall next to the Palace's big red double doors.

"That murdering, thieving, lying, dead dog eating, son of a dung beetle."

I sure was glad he wasn't looking my way as he screeched. Something was up though, and as an almost-newspaper-writer-man, I needed to find out what.

With a scant nine days before the gunfight, Gilliam Taylor, cleared out of the back room of the livery without so much as a tip or nod.

Mr. Klugmann called me to his desk, "This is a calamity! I've got journalist all over the country willing to pay for the story of a Texas gunfight between the two fastest guns around, and we're a gunfighter shy."

"Gilliam pigeon-livered out?"

"That he did. I guess he figured with the hundred he got, and a running start, the odds of him living to see Christmas were best if he didn't stay to face Waco."

"I guess, but he sure talked up a brave brag."

Klugmann said, "Come to find out, talk is all he was. Mo Fedder now says he didn't really see the gunfight between Gilliam and Apache Joe. He only came outside when he heard the shots and it was Gilliam who said it was a straight-on fair gunfight."

"Why'd Mo lie?"

"He said Gilliam threatened to kill him if he didn't, and Mo's never had much iron."

That was true.

"What happens now?" I asked, fearing my nickel a paper was drying up.

He shrugged. "The mayor and Glum are swatting hornets trying to find another gunfighter before the fourth. They asked me let every newspaper within five-hundred miles know about the $5000 prize."

"They're asking for big trouble," I said.

"How's that?" he asked.

"Polecat'll be swarming with every worthless cowboy, outlaw, and highwayman who fancies himself a fast gun. The only one getting rich in this town'll be Sampson Todd, the undertaker." I hardly got those words outa my mouth, when Sheriff Maxey came scurrying up the street from the jailhouse. "Is it true? Is it true?" He was gasping to catch more air.

"Morning, Cyrus," said Mr. Klugmann.

"You tell me right now, Friedrich. Did Leadsman tell you to advertise for gunmen to come to Polk Flat?"

"Yes, sir. I was just about to head over to the telegraph counter at the mercantile when you came puffing up."

The look the sheriff gave Mr. Klugmann could'a froze a brimstone flame. He grabbed Mr. Klugmann by the vest and pulled him to his feet. "You send that message and I'll have you in jail a'fore you can swat a fly. Mayor or not, I'm not having this town ravaged by a pack of no-goods as long as I'm wearing this here badge."

I'd never seen the boss lock-jawed before. It took a good while before he could gather a reply.

"But...I...um...yes sir...I mean, no sir. I won't, not if you don't want me to." Seemed queer, Mr. Klugmann, a man of some means in his middle fifties, saying "Sir" to a dollar-a-day fella like Cyrus Maxie.

"I wasn't thinking. You're right, sheriff. We don't need a pack of no-goods shooting up our peaceful little town."

The sheriff, turned him loose and gave him a stern nod. "You remember that."

Klugmann nodded back.

I'd never seen the sheriff so agitated. After the he left, I asked Mr. Klugmann, "What are you going to do now?" He was stuck betwixt a stampede and a wildfire.

He said, "Go tell Leadsman what the sheriff said and ask him what *he* thinks I ought to do."

"He ain't gonna like it," I told him. "Not one little bit."

"Just do it."

When I caught up with Mayor Leadsman at a back table in his saloon, he bellowed like a bogged cow. "Doesn't Maxey know I can fire him?" He reared back and let loose with a blast of cussing that would turn a gravestone red. I found out what the mop boy felt when he told the mayor that Gilliam sneaked off.

"What'cha going to do?" I asked. Klugmann would need something more for the next day's paper after he told the swollen-up story of Gilliam's cowardice.

"Tell Friedrich, the Gunfight of the Century is still on, and that we now have a more worthy and skilled gunman to match up with Waco."

I was bumfuzzled. A blink before, he was hornet-mad because Sheriff Maxey wouldn't let Klugmann put out the call, then he was all sunshine and church hymns saying he had another gunman.

I asked, "Who's going to go against Waco, Mayor?"

"It's a secret for now, but he's a dandy-do for sure. Just tell Friedrich that." He motioned for me to go, then called me back.

"Better yet, ask your boss to come see me in about an hour."

That told me Leadsman had more hiding under his hat than his bald patch.

Klugmann and the mayor met for nigh onto an hour. When he got back to the newspaper he called me inside and handed me a sealed letter. "You ride over to Ridgeville and give this to Mr. Thomas Cain at the Telegraph station there. No one else, you hear?"

I heard.

"And wait for the reply. Once you have it, you bust a bridle getting back here, and don't let on to anyone here in town about what you're doing."

"Want me to take the Wednesday stage?"

"Stage? No. Saddle up Lightening, and here's eight dollars. You can keep what's left if you get back here before six tomorrow night."

I nodded and broke for the door. Ridgeville was over twenty miles to the east as the crow flies, and I wasn't no bird.

He hollered after me, "Guard that letter. No one's to see it except Thomas Cain, the telegraph man, hear?"

"I hear," I called back, and trotted toward Fedder's Livery. Jackrabbit fast, the boss's Lightening lived ever bit up to his name. I made it to Ridgeville before sunset. The telegraph man was standing on the front stoop of his store when I rode up.

It was easy enough to find. The words Texas and New Orleans Telegraph in big black letters covered the whole side of the building. Mr. Cain flapped a mite at first, but when I handed him three dollars and the letter, he opened the station back up. He asked, "You sure you want me to send this?"

"My boss, Mr. Klugmann, is sure, and I'm his messenger." I took a gander over his shoulder as he read the message aloud.

To Ben J. Horner at the Gold Crown Saloon in Justice. Will pay $500 if you come to Polk Flat by the fourth of July and gunfight Waco Kincaid. $5000 goes to the winner of the showdown.

Just about what I'd figured. I could see how a fast gun would be sorely tempted. I asked Mr. Cain if he knew who the Horner fella was.

"Ain't you heard of Bloody Ben Horner?"

"No, Sir."

"Why he's killed a dozen men from Galveston to Dallas." The pale little man in a buckskin apron and gartered white shirt rounded his desk and sat down at the machine. He poked out the message, wagging his head the whole time. Not knowing the code, I had to trust it was as written down.

He asked, "Where you staying tonight?"

"I just rode in." I told him. "Where's a cheap, but not all bedbuggy place."

"That'll be the Hudson House. It's forty cent—no more'n four to the room, and no bugs."

Then he added, The Texas Hotel's two dollars."

"The Hudson will do."

He pointed a crooked finger toward the middle of town, "One road down that way, then turn north. You'll see it on the right. I'll send my boy over as soon I get an answer," then added,

"It won't be tonight though. I'll check at first light for the answer."

I lit out for Polecat half past sunup the next morning, Horner's reply in hand. Bloody Ben agreed to be in town by July 2ᵈ and that he'd be pleasured to kill Waco Kincaid, or anyone else for that matter, given the price promised.

***

I got back to Polecat late in the afternoon and handed the boss Bloody Ben's answer. You'd think Mr. Klugmann was shot out of an eight-gauge the way he scooted over to The Palace Saloon to give Mayor Leadsman the news. A minute later, the mayor blasted out of the Palace and down to the bank in a full run, his belly flopping like a washday shirt in a tornado. He hollered to Moss Collier, the hotel baggage man, who was toting a trunk to the stage office, "Go find Waco and tell him the gunfight is on." Moss hopped to, and headed off on his errand.

When Mr. Klugmann came back to the newspaper office he barked out orders like a prison guard. "Put on your apron. Ink the blanket. Clear the frames."

I argued I hadn't ate anything but a hardtack biscuit and a palm-sized piece of salt cod all day, but he wasn't hearing it. "I'll buy you a whole beef quarter over at Fidelia Garcia's Café when we're done."

"I'll be wanting skillet potatoes and speckledy gravy to go with it," I joshed.

He wrote the story and I set the letters as he finished each page. I was fast, Mr. Klugmann had told me so, but I'd only finished a dozen lines before he was done with the four handwritten pages.

"I'll lay the trays up for some advertisements for the backside," he said.

"You already sold some?" I asked.

"Don't worry about that. I'll run 'em now and bill 'em later. When they see tomorrow's special, they'll pay."

And pay they did. Mr. Klugmann charged eight dollars per advert and nobody squawked a little. You should've seen the stories he wrote. They were some kind of exciting, I'll tell you that, and some of them were almost true. He wrote about killings from California to Georgia just like he was standing there at the time.

The boss was good to his word about buying me supper at Fidelia's, 'sept it was breakfast the next morning. Beefsteak, potatoes, boiled onions and blackberry pudding. I'd never had a meal like that in all my days.

I lived the top-hat life that day and for quite a while after. I sold almost a thousand papers between then and the first of July when Bloody Ben Horner rode into town on a tall sorrel with silver Conchos on its saddle and breast collar.

Mr. Klugmann said, "I saw Waco go into the Palace Saloon not ten minutes ago. Go over there and tell Waco that Ben Horner's in town and see what he says." The grin on Mr. Klugmann's face was as wide as a West Texas prairie. "I'll go let the mayor know."

By sundown the next day every detail was set. Waco demanded the gunfight be moved to the south end of Main in front of the Satterfield Cotton Gin to shade the street from the evening sun, that building being the tallest in town. It took two days and nights to move the grandstands and what-not, but Waco was half of the main attraction.

Ben Horner insisted the road on that end of town be closed off. "I don't want none of Waco's worthless kin back shooting me." Of course, Mayor Leadsman and Banker Glum agreed.

By the morning of the fourth, Polecat had more souls in it than the town could hold. Main Street and every side street were blocked with wagons and ladders. Nobody was allowed into town without buying a ticket—Three dollars for men, two dollars for women, and twenty-five cents for each young'un. Even Pastor Finch joined the Merchants Association so the church would get a portion. Since the church owned little of value and took in so little, the reverend donated the church benches to be set up along the shaded side of Main Street.

Mr. Klugmann said each member of the association got a piece of the tax. One thing's for devil sure, given the size of the crowd squeezed into little Polecat on the fourth, that meant a penny a soul. Every cowpoke, farmer, barber, bather, and trader within two-hundred miles showed up for the Greatest Gunfight of the Century. Wooden toy guns, embroidered pillow cushions, and I-Saw-the-Gunfight ribbons sold like skiffs in a Noah's ark rainstorm. You can't imagine the newspapers I sold that day. They could'a filled Rattlesnake Ravine clean to the top.

The gunfighters were supposed to draw and shoot on the last ring of the church bell at six o'clock. The air was hot and dry. So many people lined the streets and side-buildings you couldn't drop a hay straw and hit the ground.

Gawkers filled every window and rooftop, and those who couldn't afford the fare, gathered on White Rock Hill a half-mile to the west.

I saw folks dressed in everything from fancy ruffles and lace to straight-from–the-field overalls. Even Sister Finch, the pastor's wife, in a brand new bonnet and shawl, perched herself on the top steps of the new church to watch.

The gunmen made one more demand, and that one suited everybody just fine, they wanted to face each other standing atop of flat-haul wagons. I guess they wanted to be in plain view for the gun draw.

Waco's pa and younger brother insisted on standing behind Waco. Pete Turnbull, Bloody Ben's cousin said, "If old man Kincaid stands behind his boy, I'm standing behind Ben."

Sheriff Maxey made both men turn in their guns. He wasn't no fool.

The two men climbed up on the wagons five minutes 'til the time. Waco's sleeves were cut off above the elbow and his holster gleamed with oil. The front of Bloody Ben Horner's holster was cut halfway down to the nose. If I were about to draw and shoot to the death, I'd want any advantage I could get too.

When the church bell gonged one, Polecat fell so quiet you could count a flea's hops on a hound's back twenty paces away.

Two! Seemed everybody's eyes were swapping back and forth, Waco to Bloody Ben, Bloody Ben to Waco, and so on.

Three! The buzz of whispers seeped from the crowd.

Four! The buzz grew louder, and a low murmur joined in.

Five! Dead quiet. An unnatural quiet. All spooky-like.

Then the sixth dong! Guns fired! Smoke and fire spit from the barrels. A blink later, shrieks and cries rose from the crowd as both men jolted back and fell still into the wagon beds. Waco lying face down with his right hand tucked under him, a huge growing red pool dripping through the wagon slat and onto the street. I looked to

Bloody Ben and his left hand resting on his lower neck, a fountain of blood oozing from between his limp fingers. Between the two, I'd never seen so much blood.

Waco's pa jumped up on the wagon and he and his other boy covered Waco with a wagon cover and dragged his carcass off toward the undertaker's parlor. At the other wagon Bloody Ben's kinfolk did much the same. As the crowd began to move in that direction, somebody at the other end of the street yelled. "Fire! Fire! The Palace is on fire!

All tarnation busted loose. The fire trough and bucket barn were less than a jackrabbit jump from Mayor Leadsman's fortune and pride, the Palace Hotel, Saloon and Gambling House. The smoke and flames swirled up the hotel's fancy white and gold porch columns and a separate fire lapped out from under the closed and locked front door of the saloon.

Ole Leadsman was nigh on to beehived, running, yelling and waving his arms something fierce. The whole town trailed close behind. So many people swarmed in the street near the Palace, the bucket line had to wiggle this way and that like a snake in on an anthill.

As Mr. Klugmann wrote in the Weekly Notice the next day, *By the time the men in the bucket line doused the fire down to soot and steam, Mayor Leadsman's elegant enterprise was entwined in rank and ruin,* but that wasn't the topline story, no sir. The topmost story was about how, while every soul in town plugged up the whole of the south end of town, some sneaky, low downs busted into the Texas Bank and Title and made off with every dollar and dime the bank had in their big iron safe.

Seems when everybody else was worried about the fire at the other end of town, somebody should have been some concerned about the bank money and the yet untallied bags of money from the day's ticket sales and the City Commerce Progress and Enrichment taxes. Even the five-thousand dollars due the winner of the gunfight was gone.

It took the rest of the evening and part of the night before the sheriff, mayor and Banker Glum, snapped to the hard notion that they had all been trapped, skinned and tanned. A throat-bled pig and bloody water bags had supplied the blood on both gunfighters and the wagons. A smitty's sledge had supplied the force taken to brake the hinges off the safe, and Clara Todd found poor Sampson, her husband, hogtied in the coffin room of his undertaker's parlor.

Word that Waco Kincaid and Ben Horner knew each other arrived in Polecat too late to stir up any suspicion. Everybody was in such a tither over the gunfight itself, they neglected to find out that Waco's ma and Ben's pa were sister and brother.

Luke Hopkins beat a near-broke Harold Leadsman in the next mayor's race 328 to 9, and the bank closed for good. It didn't make much never mind though. Folks around Polecat no longer trusted bankers and banks. I guess burying and hiding seemed a might safer.

Waco and Bloody Ben? Who knows? Texas is a mighty big place and there always seems to be plenty of gun battles to be fought and banks to rob.

About the Author

Born and raised in Central Texas, **Stan Marshall** spent his younger days enjoying football, baseball, fishing, and just about everything else a kid could do outdoors. With nearby relatives living on farms and ranched, he leaned to ride horses, brand cattle and shoot guns almost before he could walk.

Now, as in his youth, he loves all things Texas with all it offers—not only, its wide-open spaces, forests, rivers and streams, but the excitement and opportunities of its progressive big cities.

His latest book, Half the Distance, a contemporary young adult novel, published by Hartwood Publishing, tells the story of a Texas high school boy plucked from the big city and rudely deposited in a small tight-knit rural community in the Texas Hill Country.
The story contains many elements of the author's own experiences as a teen.

Now living in Cypress on the outskirts of Houston, he's married to his college sweetheart, with three beautiful daughters and one very spoiled grandson. Stan enjoys Texas alright, but most of all, he loves family, friend, and writing.

Four Days in the Texas Hill Country

By Mary Jo Martin

Four Days in the Texas Hill Country

DAVID TOLD ME for years: "You can learn to love them." I always replied, "Not a chance. They look evil and smell bad." I'm a city girl, born and bred. My family lived in Philadelphia for 200 years before I arrived. I was doomed. My idea of nature was the single sycamore tree on our city block, plus the bachelor buttons and nasturtiums I planted in our minuscule backyard. Fifty-three years ago, I met and later married a boy from a small town in western Pennsylvania. He convinced me to try camping with mixed results. We hiked in the woods with handguns and rifles, shooting cans and bottles, while generally observing nature. Those experiences taught me what the natural world is.

    My country mouse, David, and I recently visited the Texas Hill Country for four days. We rented a cabin near the Sabinal River, on the Edwards Plateau, close to a place called Lost Maples State Natural Area. Although semi-arid, it was lush along the river banks, filled with large-leaved sycamores and Uvalde Bigtooth Maples that are unique to that location. Add to that wildflowers, butterflies, and birds in abundance. In autumn, the maples' leaves turn bright red and gold. It's one of the few places in Texas where you can see what Fall looks like.

    We were totally off the grid. No TV, marginal Wi-Fi, and no phone service. The nearest town—Vanderpool—was a half-hour drive south. Fifteen more minutes to the south was the bigger town of Utopia. If we wanted to go to the "big city" of Bandera with grocery and hardware stores, we had to devote an hour's time. Twice that round trip.

What is one to do in this lovely place? Read on the porch, watch birds from the bird blind in the park, eat, sleep, and actually have conversations. With a left knee recuperating from arthroscopic surgery, I couldn't hike, so that was out. Besides, Central Texas swelters in late June. I sweat very easily and hate it.

We soon discovered that the owners of the property had chickens. Although I love birds, chickens are not my favorites. My first encounter with them was at a county fair in Ohio. They were crowded into small pens. Seeing them like that was unpleasant and smelly, unlike visiting the cows or pigs. Although those animals didn't have great aromas, they were at least fun to watch and had pretty eyes.

On our second day, the chickens came to visit. When I saw them, I remarked, "Oh, good grief, chickens!" I also reminded David of my feelings towards these fowls, "They have beady little eyes. And they smell ungodly awful."

Unlike me, David was thrilled. He's always wanted to be a chicken owner. Suburban neighborhoods have deed restrictions that prohibit them. Fine by me.

Even with their beady little eyes, I admitted they were fun to watch. There were two roosters and four hens. One of the roosters was the alpha—a big bully. But he was very protective of his three hens. I named them Henry VIII, Hortense, Henrietta, and Honey. Henrietta was the independent one. She'd go off on her own in search of bugs—or whatever—leaving Henry, Hortense, and Honey to go their collective way.

David laughed at my names for them, saying, "I know you like them. Otherwise you wouldn't be giving them names."

The other rooster was definitely the inferior, even though he was much more handsome than Henry VIII. He had striped tail feathers, and his iridescent plumes glistened in the sun, changing colors as he moved. I named him Edward. He shepherded one hen, a beautiful mottled grey girl I called Elizabeth. I suppose these groups were what you might call "cluck-cliques."

We'd bought black-oil sunflower seeds to feed the songbirds at the park, but put them out for the chickens every day. Of course, we had repeat visits, since we fed them.

On the last day we were there, I was reading by myself on the porch, when I had a surprise. A big surprise. Out from behind the chicken coop came the largest rooster I'd ever seen. He stood close to four feet tall. This convinced me. Birds had indeed evolved from dinosaurs. I hoped he didn't have velociraptor teeth. Not only was he huge, but he could speak! It started with a series of clucks, then transformed into English.

He introduced himself with a small bow "Hello, my name is James, and I am the most unique chicken you will ever see."

What could I say? I gulped, and stammered, "You certainly are unusual, James. And quite handsome." He scratched at the ground. Likely a bit embarrassed, or pleased at the compliment.

He asked, "So, what is this belief you have that chickens smell foul? And have beady little eyes?"

"Well, my only experience with chickens before this weekend was at a county fair." "Hmmmph. No wonder you had that impression. Those chickens are bred to be stupid and lazy, and they don't take good care of themselves. No wonder they smelled bad. As for eyes, step a little closer and look at mine."

I wasn't sure just how close I wanted to get—with visions in my mind about Jurassic Park and those velociraptors—but I didn't want to hurt his feelings. So, I moved up to see his eyes better. They were spectacular. The color of a beautiful, clear Texas sky, with a hint of gold flecks.

"Wow!" I said, "I see what you mean. You are indeed a special creature. And you don't smell bad either."

At that, he scratched the ground again. And I swear, he smiled. He turned away to go back to the coop, and called, "Please remember me when you start to think badly of chickens."

"Of course! This has been unforgettable." After he was gone, David came out of the cabin and said, "Hi! What have you been doing?"

"You will not believe this, but I just met a four-foot tall talking rooster." "Right." He rolled his eyes. "Just as you fell asleep while you were reading and dreamed the whole thing. I know things are bigger in Texas, but that's hard to swallow."

"Go behind the chicken coop and see if you don't find him." David, being a good sport, went behind the chicken coop. He came back laughing so hard, he could barely walk straight. "Did you know that our hosts have kids?"

"No. I've never seen them." "Well, there's at least one, and he's dressed in a beautiful rooster suit. He told me his name is James and that he just scared an old lady. He thought it was hysterical."

"I'm not sure how hysterical I think it was, but I guess he did fool me." All of the laughter brought James's mom out. We told her the story, and she laughed, too. After she apologized to me.

I told her, "Don't worry about it. This will give me a tall tale to tell."

After years of saying how much I disliked chickens, that trip taught me to learn to love them. Well, maybe a bit. Except for James, I still think they have beady little eyes, but at least they don't smell bad.

Whether you're a kid or a tourist, when you don't have much else to do in rural Texas, you find your entertainment where you can.

About the Author

Mary Jo Martin, is an award-winning writer who lives in the suburbs of Houston, Texas. She is a member of the Houston Writer's Guild. Her short story about a poisoning, Flowers for Lewis, was published in the Houston Writer's Guild Press anthology, Waves of Suspense (2015).

A personal medical mystery led her on a quest to find her father's medical history.

Instead, she discovered a huge family. This work, Sibling Revelries, won first place in the memoir category in a Houston Writer's Guild contest.

Mary Jo started her professional life as a chemist. Along the way, she got an MBA, and practiced marketing and market research for forty years. After years of doing concise business writing, she is now free to do "real" writing.

Too Darn Friendly

Adopted by Jim "from Texas" Matej

Too Darn Friendly

YEP, IT'S TRUE...Texas is a mighty friendly place. Now mind you, we have our share of people who can be considered the south end of a north bound horse—and some are just as smart. But on the whole, if you smile at a local down here they will be happy to smile back. If you stop one and ask directions, they will be as helpful as they can. We even have some who are so friendly they would strike up a conversation with a fence post if nothing else was around. The latter is what I figured I had come across in Hobby Airport a few years back.

It was a long flight from where-ever-it was-I-was-coming-back-from. After several unexpended delays, another soft drink and several extra bags of peanuts, I had some pressing business to attend to first thing upon my arrival.

You see, using the "facilities" on an airplane during flight is unnerving to me for some reason. Somehow, the sound of air screaming past the fuselage at 500 miles per hour and the possibility of flying into rampaging air turbulence makes for a very intense experience – especially in the venerable position of sitting with your pants down. I just know that with the slightest rivet failure or inadvertent flush I could be sucked out of the airplane though the toilet.

I don't know why, but free falling thirty-thousand feet with my pants down around my ankles and naked backside exposed to all of creation is just not how I what to leave this life. But then, I guess this is just a little phobia of mine that you're probably are not really interested in hearing about.

As I rounded the corner into an airport restroom and hurried into the first empty stall, a sense of relief came over me. I was barely sitting down when I heard a voice from the other stall saying in a long, slow Texas drawl: "Hi, how are ya?"

Shocked at hearing the question, I looked over in the direction of the voice. But what even shocked me more is that I responded, somewhat embarrassed, "Well... doin' just fine!"

I bent down as far as I could to look into the next stall and saw these shiny new cowboy boots with a brand new pair of blue jeans draped over them. My first thought was, "Oh Lordy, Bubba Bob's done come to town." I would have been willing to bet that he was sitting there wearing his cowboy hat too.

Then he says: "So, what are ya up to?"

Alright! That's just too darn friendly if you ask me. But apparently unaccustomed to big city restroom etiquette, I figured he didn't mean any harm and was just being a good ol' boy. So in an effort to be neighborly I said, "Uhh, like you, just traveling!"

In my mind's eye I could see Buddha Bob down on the farm, sitting in an outhouse, talking to the cows and chickens as they passed by.

I'm now concentrating on finishing my business in order to get out as fast as I can when I heard another question. "Can I come over?"

OKAY, good ol' boy or not, that question just crossed the line.

As politely as I could I tried to bluntly end the conversation by saying, "No! I'm kind of busy right now."

Then his thick Texas accent took on a perturbed sound as he said, "Listen, I'll have to call ya back. There's an idiot in the next stall answering all my questions!" I don't think I have ever been quieter in my life than during the next few minutes. As the other fella exited his stall I just sat. I didn't hear anyone else enter the restroom and I didn't make any attempt to leave. I wanted to make sure that my new friend not only had time to leave the restroom but the airport terminal entirely.

As I sat there in my solitude, I became painfully aware that I was now officially included in that share of Texans who strikingly resemble the south end of a north bound horse—and I felt just as smart too.

About the Author

Jim Matej: The simple facts.
James Matej; born 8/12/1950 in East Bernard, Texas
After that the facts gets a little more complicated. As I guess they do for all of us.

You might have noticed a discrepancy in the above; that discrepancy is why I am here. I still use James as my business name—it's a numerology thing. I went by it most of my life, but in realizing that I had totally screwed-up that life I decided to spend the rest of my years as Jim. You see, I came into this world a trombone player and was given the talent, desire and opportunities to become one of the best in the world. My heart and soul was music and in my youth I became a successful freelance trombonist earning a living by just playing music in the Houston area.

Then my heart was distracted and I got married. When the kids started popping out I had to bury my music deep in my soul in order to honestly fulfill my duties as husband and father. Unfortunately that's all over now and I sit here looking at the latter years of my life with my musical talent and desire still burning inside me. But my opportunities of becoming a successful professional musician are in the past. So I said to myself, *Hey, I know what... I'll become a writer!*

Legacy Ranch Scrapbook

By Carol and William Mays

LEGACY RANCH SCRAPBOOK

SYLVIA GARCIA PETERSON rifled through her purse before she went into Shady Oaks Retirement Home. Counting the change, she had a few pennies less than 25 dollars. Paying for lunch for her and her mother, Maria, would take at least 10 or 11, even if they ate kids' meals at Whataburger. That didn't leave much for shopping or to feed her son that evening. She wouldn't eat lunch. She would get her mother something to eat, and say she was dieting. She was too fat, anyway. Maybe if she hadn't let herself get fat, she'd still have a husband.

Shady Oaks was a miserable place. Located in Corpus Christi on the forgotten side town, it was the last stop before death if you were old and poor. And to make matters worse it was Texas-themed. From the rusting Lone Star to all the cowboy pictures on the walls everything reminded her of her ex-husband Bryce.

Residents were parked in their wheelchairs in the dingy hallways. One elderly man slept on a gurney next to a public restroom. The stench of urine and bleach emanated from all the rooms, and the worst smell came from a room where a woman screamed dangling off her bed. The workers never moved to help her. Sylvia yelled at them, but they ignored her, so she walked into the room and helped the woman back on the bed.

"Thank you, my dear," the woman said.

Sylvia's mother was right next door. "Ola, mama!" she said, trying to sound as cheerful as possible, as if their lives hadn't completely fallen apart.

Sylvia felt horrible. Not only did Bryce break her heart when he ran off with his girlfriend, he had destroyed her parents too.

They had trusted him when they plunked down their life savings for the down payment on the home in the Royal Grace Subdivision where they would all live together. Her father couldn't take it when the bank foreclosed. His heart had been failing for years anyway.

"I have thought of the perfect thing for us to do today. Going to garage sales." Sylvia tried to sound enthusiastic, like it was trip to Disneyland instead of the only thing they could afford.

Her mother didn't seem fooled. "Si. Vamanos," she said in a sad voice.

Sylvia wheeled her out of the room and past the smirking nurses.

Her mother scolded them in a loud voice. "God watches everything you do. And everything you *don't do!*"

The nurses glared back, and that made Sylvia feel a little better. But would they be mean to Maria later when she was alone in her room?

Desperate for something good to happen, Sylvia stopped at the first garage sale, but as soon as she got out of the car, she wanted to jump back in and drive off. There was a pair of boots, fancy with some rhinestones. And a saddle, and oil paintings of cowboys on horses. It all reminded her of Bryce. Even though she was Hispanic, and he was Anglo, they had many things in common. They had grown up in the Texas countryside and both of them were Catholic. She remembered how handsome he had looked in his camouflage outfit when he went hunting. How could he have let her and her parents drain their savings for the down payment on the house when all along he had been having an affair and was planning to leave her?

"Mama, let's go," she said.

Her mother, who had barely been able to walk when she left the nursing home, had made it out of the car on her own, and was standing at a table looking at a book. That was unusual. Sylvia raced over to her.

"Look, mija," Maria said with excitement, pointing at a scrapbook full of old black and white pictures. "I want this." Sylvia flipped through the pages. It was thick, dusty, -- and strange. The photos were quite old. They showed scenes from farms and ranches. Men on horses. Women quilting. In one photo a Model-T was parked next to a barn.

"How old is this?" Sylvia asked, as much to herself as her mother.

Maria's eyes glittered. There was more life in them than she had seen in a while. "I want it," she repeated.

It was on a table with a note that said all items were a dollar. What a bargain. Such a small price to pay for making her mother happy. The woman running the sale walked over to them. Sylvia handed her the dollar, and she took it.

"Do you know anything about this?" Sylvia asked her.

"Not much. My parents were antique dealers, and this was something they had in their store. I have no idea where it came from." She motioned to all the other items around her. "A lot of their stuff came from the farms and ranches around here."

"Who are the people in these photos?"

The woman took the book and leafed through it. "I don't know any of these people. My parents told me that some of these old photos dated as far back as the 1890s. I did some research.

The Kodak camera wasn't available until then, so these would have been some of the first pictures taken in this area. I think they were taken at our local ranch just outside Corpus Christi.

You may know it -- Legacy Ranch? My parents found it there, I think. They handled the estate sale for the ranch when the owners died. But honestly, I don't know much about this scrapbook.

It was in my parents' store for years, and it never sold. Customers would come into the store and look at it for hours. Older people. But no one ever bought it. Strange, huh?"

As the woman leafed through the book, she got a funny look on her face. "Hey, something's not right. I think there are more pictures than they're used to be." She stopped talking and looked bug-eyed at one of the pictures. "I don't think I can sell this to you."

"I want it," Maria said. The woman shoved the dollar back toward Sylvia. "Here's your dollar back. Plus, I'll give you anything else off the dollar table that you want."

Maria shook her head. "I want it."

"No, no, I can't let it go."

"I want it," Maria wailed.

Why would the woman back out of the sale? Probably because she was letting it go too cheap. All the other customers turned to look. The woman was momentarily distracted, and Sylvia snatched it out of her hand. How dare she try to take that scrapbook away from her mother? "A deal is a deal. You had it on the dollar table. I gave you a dollar. You can't take it back."

"But, but," the woman sputtered.

Sylvia turned and walked away, pushing her mother in front of her. Maria took the scrapbook, and she smiled and thumbed through it all the way to Whataburger and all the way back to Shady Oaks. She was still smiling the next week then Sylvia came to visit. And she was still looking at the scrapbook.

"Come on, mama, let's get out of here for a while."

"No thanks, mija. I just want to sit here and look at the scrapbook."

Sylvia thought the book was Maria's way of coping with her horrid, new surroundings, and she was delighted to see her mother happy. Besides, she was flat broke, not even five dollars in her purse. The Catholic Church had given her a job teaching at a middle school after the divorce, but payday was almost a week away, and she was overjoyed not to spend any money.

The next Saturday, paycheck in hand, she found her mother sitting with the scrapbook again. She refused to go out, and Sylvia started to worry that the scrapbook was turning into an obsession.

All week she couldn't concentrate at work. The students looked at her with blank expressions. She had trouble remembering what she had said, and what she was supposed to say next. Deciding to see what her mother was up to during the week, she skipped her lunch hour and asked one of the other teachers to cover for her if she came back late. When she got to Shady Oaks, she sneaked down the corridor and opened the door to Maria's room without knocking. As she'd feared, Maria sat there with the scrapbook.

"Mama, you're spending all your time with that."

"It makes me happy. It's where I want to live forever."

Sylvia tried to dismiss it as a mental escape-- a type of coping mechanism her mother had developed. But she kept worrying. That Wednesday she skipped morning mass and tiptoed to the door to her mother's room. Maria was talking to someone. Carrying on a conversation. But no one was answering.

When she pushed the door open, she found Maria by herself in her vinyl recliner with the open scrapbook in her lap.

"Who were you talking to mama?"

Maria did not answer which was unusual for her. She just stared at the scrapbook almost as if in a trance. And it seemed to have more pictures and pages than Sylvia had remembered.

That was exactly what the lady at the yard sale had said! Feeling a chill of fear, she ran out of the room to the nurses' station.

"I need to talk to someone about my mother."

One of the nurses looked up with a smirk. "Which room?" she asked in a nasal voice.

She knew which room her mother was in. How horrible she was acting. Sylvia was about to yell at them, but the phone rang and the nurse answered. It was a personal call, and their conversation droned on. Sylvia glanced around. A young college student who was interning there looked back at her with what seemed like sympathy. Sylvia walked over to her.

"Could you help me?" She looked at the intern's name tag, "Darlene, is it?"

Darlene looked around nervously. None of the nurses were paying any attention.

"Could you keep an eye on my mother and call me if she does anything unusual. She's the one in Room 166."

Darlene nodded, and then hesitated. "I know which one she is. She talks in her room all the time. Like she's carrying on a conversation. The nurses think she's senile. But she seems pretty sharp."

"Please, please, help me."

"I can't. They have all kind of rules."

Sylvia wrote down her name and cell phone number on a piece of paper. "Please call me day or night."

Darlene crossed her arms. No one had a good heart in this miserable place. There were no favors done for anyone -- ever! Sylvia resorted to the only thing left: money. She had just cashed her paycheck and had fifty dollars left after paying her bills and buying some – but not all – of her groceries. She would have to ask for food from the church pantry. She just fell another rung down the ladder of life.

She thrust the money in Darlene's hand. "I can pay you more if you call me."

Darlene looked side to side and shoved the money into her pocket.

Sylvia planned to go back to Shady Oaks the next day, but when she got home, her son had a high fever. He had caught the flu, and she had to stay home with him. When he got well, Sylvia had to catch up with grading papers and volunteer extra shifts at St. Mary's to repay the church for all their kindness and generosity. Then, her son had several basketball games, and Sylvia attended all of them to make up for the boy's absent father.

One night as a blue norther blew into Corpus Christi, Sylvia's phone rang.

It was the nasal-voiced nurse. "Sylvia Garcia-Peterson?"

Sylvia knew it was bad news. "Yes."

"We are very sorry to inform you that your mother is missing."

Sylvia bolted upright. "Missing? What do you mean?"

"The security guard was making his rounds," she stammered. "He heard a man's voice in the room with your mother."

Sylvia trembled. "A man's voice? What man?" Could it be her ex-husband, Bryce?

"No one was admitted into the building past six this evening. Your mother had her dinner with the rest of the residents in the dining room. Darlene, one of our interns, said she heard your mother telling the other residents at the table that she was going away to a beautiful place. No one thought anything of it, because residents say things like that. But, when the security guard heard a man's voice in the room, he was concerned. He tried to open the door, but couldn't. We've called the police and would like it if you could come here right now."

Sylvia left her son a note on the kitchen table. It was better not to wake him. Where could her mother be? Why hadn't Darlene called her? Thankful that she did not live in New York or San Francisco or any other crowded city in the United States, she sped off in the dead of night down the deserted streets.

When she arrived, no one was there to greet her. The nurse's station was empty. A janitor mopping the floor knew nothing about her mother or police, merely mumbled something about being the only person working during shift change.

Anger spiked inside her, then yielded to fear.

She slowly pushed the door to her mother's room open. No one was there. The scrapbook lay on the night stand open to the last page. The large black and white photo showed a picnic in an open field on a sunny day. It was captioned "Legacy Ranch Annual Picnic 1875."

Sylvia had seen all the pictures in the scrapbook, but this was new. There were a hundred people all smiling. They were seated at one long wooden table under a large oak tree. The table was covered with all kinds of delicious foods in iron pots and pans. There was cornbread, barbeque and a pot of pinto beans that Sylvia thought looked just like the kind her mother made with the jalapenos in it. Men, women, and children all sat together happy and smiling. The women wore cotton prairie style dresses and sun bonnets. The men wore cowboy hats, boots and guns in holsters. A cattle dog sat next to a little boy.

Suddenly, she could hear happy voices. It sounded like a party. Some were speaking Spanish, others English. A cowboy played a guitar and sang, "Home on the Range."

The smell of the food wafted up to her. That startled her so much she almost dropped the scrapbook. Then the people started to move, like a video. Sylvia stood motionless. How could this be happening? She felt faint as the images became more three-dimensional. They came loose from the page and floated around her. They were translucent.

One young woman floated in front of her wearing a cross like her mother had. "I'm fine,

Mija," the woman said. "Don't worry."

It was her mother for sure, but when she was young, barely in her twenties. Next to her, another familiar-looking woman waved at Sylvia. Who was she? She moved next to her mother and smiled.

It was the woman who had held the garage sale.

Sylvia felt light-headed and started to faint. The scrapbook slipped out of her hand and fell into a large crack which opened up in the wall and foundation.

Now, it waits for the next person to wish as hard as they can to live somewhere else in a place far away in a time that even *time* has forgotten.

About the Author

Carol Mays and William Mays are both writers. Together they co-wrote Escape from Sunny Shores, a novel about senior citizens who prison break a nursing home. Carol also authored a self-help book, 103 Crazy Ideas for Surviving Suburbia, and is currently working on a children's book, Nevins the Cat. William wrote a mob book, Family Obligations, and has released a photography book, The View from Oso Creek, and is currently working on the sequel to Family Obligations.

A Path Best Unwalked
By Derpy_Girl

A Path Best Unwalked

Walking home,
With my phone in hand,
Talking to my dad.

 I stepped into the dog park,
The gate closed behind,
I started the long walk to the other side.

The path made of gravel, the tiny pebble, stuck in my shoe,
I paid attention to every move,
Every step I took,
Along this path.

Unsuspecting, I followed my route,
Right in the mouth of a beast,
His teeth never managed to pierce my skin,
But he did bark and bite, nip,
Clawing at my skin,
Protected by my long jeans, hand-me downs, denim worn,

I kept walking, picking up the pace,
Trying to escape, calm and yet shaken,
But then he jumped up,
Snapping at my arms, never relenting in his task,

I came to a stop…
I turned to the dog, fearing the last assault,
It reared and lunged for me

About to hurt me bad,
Luckily, it's owner came and tugged him away.

The woman never once said sorry or even glanced at me at all,

As if it was nothing.
As if I was nothing.

I walked away,
Acting calm,

My dad still on the phone,
Yelling concerns at me.
I stepped out of the park.

I was free.

About the Author

Derpy_Girl is a high school sophomore at YES Prep Northbrook High School and was inspired by her English teacher, Ms. Jasmine Britton, to explore and find herself as a writer.

Time by the Sea

By Kate Mock

Time by the Sea

THE MUFFLED SOUND first woke Becky up. And in that moment she panicked; the memories from the night before blurry and difficult to recall. What happened? Why couldn't she remember?

Throwing off the blankets she found herself alone in a room decorated with pale colors that seemed old yet comforting. She woke up in a long-sleeve shirt and loose cotton sweatpants. This certainly wasn't what she was wearing last night. Becky wasn't even sure she owned any clothing like this. It intensified her confusion, what had she been doing?

The answer teased the edge of her mind but refused to come out. Her current attempts to use make her brain work it out only started a headache. Conceding defeat for the moment, Becky opened the bedroom door.

A short hallway led her to the living area which combined the kitchen and living room into one. Sunlight came from the far end of the area through windows and a glass paned door. The muffled sound came from there.

She rubbed her upper arms while walking toward that door and the sound beyond. Something coated the glass making it hard to see through. The knob proved stubborn but eventually gave away and opened. The bright sunlight made Becky flinch until her eyes adjusted. She stood on a small balcony several feet up. Directly below her were a couple of other balconies like the one she was on and a steep drop that led to a beach. The vastness of the ocean had been beyond what she ever thought about before but now...

An expanse of gray-blue stretched out to touch the sky far away. The water closer to the beach was mottled with white as the waves glomped the sand. Breathing through her mouth Becky tasted the salt in the air. A slight breeze toyed her hair, floating them above her shoulders.

Her hands were shaking as she stepped back inside and slammed the door closed, the view too much for her to handle right now.

Back inside instinct told her something in the room changed during her brief time on the balcony. Slowly she turned around and saw it immediately. Arrange on the coffee table were four objects. For some reason, seeing them caused a lump of dread to form in her stomach. Sliding down to the floor, Becky tried to make sense of the emotional whirlpool consuming her. She didn't even notice she wasn't alone until someone put a hand on her head.

"I thought you'd be okay on your own but it looks like I underestimated how hard this would be for you." Raising her head, Becky found herself scrutinized by a pair of the bluest eyes she'd ever seen.

"Who are you?" she whispered.

The other woman smiled, "My name is Callie, dear."

"Where…"

"A condo in a lovely place called Galveston. My first time here was on vacation a few years ago. I'd live here all year long if I wasn't scared of the hurricanes. You needn't worry about that, that season is months away. Of course, I brought you here."

"Why?"

Callie's expression grew serious and she knelt down so her eyes were on level as Becky's. "You got yourself into some trouble, Becky. You're here to sort it out. Then you can go home."

"But I don't remember what happened."

"That's all right. It'll come to you soon. Right now, just focus on you."

"What?"

"Once you figure that out," Callie said, "the rest will come."

Still confused, Becky was pulled up by Callie who proceeded to brush and straighten Becky's outfit. The girl jerked her arms away from Callie's well-meaning fingers. The woman acted like she didn't notice the action.

"It's pretty lonely out here so there won't be anything to distract you."

"What about you? Why are you here?" Becky asked.

"Well, if you need someone to vent at or a sympathetic ear to listen, I'll never be too far away."

Becky returned the smile half-heartedly and looked for something else to focus her attention on. The only things readily available occupied the coffee table. Swallowing her fear for another time she sat down on the loveseat and took her time looking them over. There was nothing inherently scary or off-putting about them individually; but something about seeing them all together upset her. But how? How could a sewing kit, a plush cat, a compass, and a hand mirror make her feel like this?

"What is it, Becky?"

"I…" She grabbed the toy cat and clutched it tightly to her chest. "I'm not sure. There's something familiar about these things."

"Not surprising. Each of them has a deep meaning to you. And before you ask, you have to figure that out for yourself," Callie said. "Once you've done that, then you'll be able to move on. Start with that cat, why don't ya?" The woman left the girl there and stepped out to the balcony.

The wind was picking up, and it looked like a storm was forming on the horizon. She sighed. Dammit, this was going to be harder than she thought it would. While this place came from Callie's memories of a wonderful trip here, Becky's stormy feelings matched the foreboding weather. She didn't get why. So right now things weren't looking too good.

Callie wasn't going to give up yet. Yes, this was the first time she tried this treatment on someone like Becky; a lot could still go wrong. She was certain this would work and Becky was the perfect candidate to prove it.

A glance back inside showed Becky wasn't hurting herself; she was just curled up in the loveseat, the cat still held to her chest. Callie bit her lip, undecided on what to do. It was always a delicate balancing act, knowing when to intervene and when to step back. She finally decided it was better to talk with Becky than allow her to continue stewing like this. She entered the living room and took the chair positioned at a right angle to the loveseat.

"Are you okay, dearie? Have you anything you want to talk about?" When Becky shrugged, Callie just sat quietly, waiting.

"It's just…" the girl sighed. "I really wish I could remember, you know. That would make everything so much easier."

"They'll come back as you figure things out. I promise. The items on the coffee table are meant to help."

"How?" Becky asked.

"You tell me. Each of them holds some kind of significance to you. We'll figure out what that is together." She pointed at the cat. "Let's start with that"

The girl studied the plush toy a moment then hugged it again. "It…it reminds me of someone."

"Who?" Callie chuckled at the girl's discomfort. "Someone you have a crush on?"

"Y-yeah. A boy I met after, after my father got custody of me. The way he acts sometimes kinda reminds me of a cat."

"Really? Is that all?"

"He also won me a toy cat just like this one at the State Fair." The girl sniffed and pressed the heel of her right hand against her eyes. "I wish I hadn't been so mean to him."

"What did you do?"

"We, we got into an argument the last time we saw each other. And…"

"And you said some things you regret? Oh, honey, a lot of people have arguments like that when they're young. But I'm sure the two of you can work it out if you're both willing. Can I ask you something?"

"Sure."

"What was the argument about?"

Becky shifted her position in the loveseat slightly before she explained. The main sore point of contention between them was her adoration for her maternal grandmother, a former theater actress, would be a better guardian than her father. "He didn't even know I existed until Social Services contacted him after Mom died," he said.

Callie could guess where this narrative was going. She refrained from voicing her assumptions; she could be wrong, despite what five years of doing this said otherwise. Still she stayed silent; Becky needed to talk it out.

So the girl explained that the last argument had been the crush's final attempt to talk her out of running away to be with her grandmother. "But I was determined to go."

"Was living with your dad really that bad?" Callie asked. This was something she needed cleared up.

"Actually not really. I just didn't feel like I belong there, you know."

"And was living with your grandmother everything you hoped for?"

"It seemed like that first," Becky replied slowly. "But maybe I was just ignoring everything that screamed I should stay put. I discovered my grandmother cared more about her reputation and appearance than my welfare. That was the reason why Mom never introduced us. How could I have been so stupid?"

Callie patted her shoulder to calm her down. "I wouldn't say stupid," she said. "Naïve maybe."

Becky sobbed, "And now I have nowhere else to go."

"Why do you say that?"

"Gr-grandmother told me that after running away like I did, there's no way Dad would want me back. So I had to stay with her."

"Do you know that for a fact, did you hear your father say this?"

"N-no."

"Then don't be so quick to take her word for it," Callie said. "Maybe your father is waiting for you to go back to him. Maybe he's worried sick about you and wants to know you're okay. Have you tried calling him?"

Becky shook her head, too upset to use words. Callie squeezed her hard. "Then, hey, maybe your grandmother's wrong about your dad."

"And if she's right?"

"Don't worry about something like that right now. Let's focus on other things." Callie looked at the coffee table. "What's with the sewing basket? Do you do a lot of sewing?"

The girl needed a moment to regain her composure. "My mom did a lot of sewing to help make some extra cash. She had a lot of patience teaching me how to do it when I got old enough. Wasn't long before I was sewing right beside her." She choked out a laugh, "Even got better than her after a few years."

It must be a happy memory by the way the girl smiled. A couple of sniffles later and Becky sat up straighter.

Callie leaned forward, "Becky?"

"I just remembered something," Becky said.

"What is it?"

"My, my dad was interested in my sewing and encouraged me to learn new techniques and challenge myself. He was even going to find me a teacher." Burying her face in her hands, Becky cried, "I've been an idiot. He wanted me to feel more at home by taking an interest in my hobbies and talents."

"Perhaps he might be willing to take you back if you ask him," Callie responded. That calmed the girl down. Callie snuck a peek outside. There was still a storm on the horizon; but it wasn't as looming as it had been earlier. She was relieved, they were making progress. Callie was positive the grandmother was the toxic element resulting in Becky's current state. Restoring the girl to her father's care was the best solution. But there was one more thing to do before she could consider this session closed.

"Becky?"

"Yeah?"

"What's the deal with the mirror?"

In the distance, thunder rumbled as the girl stared at the object. The expression on her face told Callie she needed to tread carefully here. Whatever this object represented, it held a lot of negative connotations for Becky.

"Why does it have to mean anything?" the girl replied. She turned away, clearly uncomfortable. And doing her best to avoid looking at the mirror.

"Come on, Becky, I told you the rules. Everything on the coffee table means something to you, including the mirror. So come on, why is it so important?"

"Because it reminds me of her!" Becky shouted, competing with the sudden storm outside.

"Who?" Callie asked though the answer was obvious. "Your grandmother?"

Becky nodded, "There's a full-size mirror with the exact same design as the hand mirror hanging in her house. It dated back from Grandmother's time in the theater. She loved that damn thing. It's her prized possession. She'd spend hours polishing it to a shine and always, always checked her reflection in it before leaving the house for any reason. Even for minor stuff like checking the mailbox." The girl shifted in her seat. "She certainly didn't like anyone else touching that mirror."

Callie leaned forward in sympathy. This old woman was definitely the primary toxic element in the girl's environment. A restraining order and removal of all legal rights to Becky should be considered. She sat back when she noticed Becky plucking the ends of her sleeves.

"What is it?" she asked quietly.

"I...I remember being so mad at her, like there was something that was a final straw. And I was done; I was done with her. But I hurt a lot inside. I think I reached a point where I was giving up on, on everything. So I..." Words dying on her lips, Becky set the toy cat next to her and slowly pulled the sleeves of her shirt back to the elbow. Across both wrists were ugly red gashes.

"I wanted to hurt her, let her know what it's like to be under her thumb. So I broke her precious mirror. And...and then I used the largest of the glass shards on myself." After pulling the sleeves down, Becky looked straight at Callie. "Am I dead? Is this Hell?"

Callie chuckled and ruffled the girl's hair. "No, no, sweetie, you're not dead. You came close though. Fortunately you were found before too much blood was lost."

"Found? By who? I was alone in the house."

Callie smiled, "Why don't I make things a bit clearer?"

"What do you mean?"

"Right now you're lying in a hospital in a medically induced coma. This entire experience is part of a treatment for those who have attempted suicide. Therapists like me want to help patients like you find a resolution to the pain you're in; find an alternative to ending your life." She leaned forward to the coffee table and handed Becky the compass. "So what do you choose? Are you willing to work with me to move beyond this or do you want to simply let all this go?" Rhythmic beeping got her attention first. It reminded Becky of something, but she wasn't sure what. Maybe something she saw on TV a few times. Her eyes opened to a dim hospital room. An outside window said it was night. An attempt to sigh brought on a coughing fit and woke up the other occupant in the room.

"Becky? Baby, are you okay? I mean, well, damn, I'm not good at this."

A lamp in the corner flicked on and struggling to stand out of a recliner was her father. She forced herself to stay quiet and take deep breaths. Soon she was sipping water through a straw held by him.

"Easy, easy, sweetie. You were out for almost a week."

Carefully she touched his stubble covered cheek in

amazement. Had he stayed here by her side the whole time? She wrinkled her nose, judging by the odor most likely.

He laughed at her expression. "Yeah, yeah, I could stand to use a shower. But I wanted to be here when you woke up."

They smiled at each other, tears silently rolling down their cheeks

About the Author

Kate Mock, while born a West Point army brat in New York State, quickly adapted to Texas living and can't think of any other (real world) place she would rather be. She currently lives in Dallas with her husband and two cats and dabbles in the scary world of self-published e-books.

Not So Wonderful
By David Welling

Not So Wonderful

THE BARTENDER PAUSED, then slid the whiskey shot across the bar. "You may want to slow down a bit. Let me get you a glass of water."

"I don't need no fuggin' water. Just keep em' coming." Tony held the glass to the light, studying the reflection in the amber liquid. "Charge it to my room." He took a sizable gulp, relishing the scorch that ran down his throat. Medicine for the traumatized.

The bartender stood at attention, mouth open and ready to offer a response—most likely to do with limits. Then, apparently thinking better, put a zipper on it.

"Doesn't matter anyway. I'm not driving anywhere, so you can get off your professional responsibility high horse." Tony cast a glance around the near-empty hotel bar, a couple seated in an isolated corner, chatting quietly. At the far end of the bar to his left, two women sat, talking about God knows what. His eyes met one and he raised his glass in salute. "Ladies," he greeted. She turned her head. He returned his attention to the bartender. "What's your name, son?"

"Bernie."

"Well... Bernie..." He tapped his glass. "This is one thing that never disappoints."

"Staying long?" The bartender's tone suggested he hoped not.

A snort, filled as much with sarcasm as alcohol slipped out. "I've no fuggin' idea. This is my home now. Lost my own... and everything else.

Bernie nodded. "From the flood?" A common story, people displaced from too much rain at one time, in a region prone to storms. The gulf coast offered infinite varieties of flooding opportunities.

"Nah. That woulda been too easy." Tony grinned, flashing five decades of coffee stains across his teeth. "I earned my expulsion, but it was one hell of a good ride, every last one. Now, I got no home, my wife's gone, friends, business deals, kids, they don't want to talk to me." He took another slurp.

Bernie's eyes darted to past his customer, as if looking for a quick exit. No use.

"You know the word, 'pariah?'" The bartender shook his head in response. Tony pulled his phone and tapped the screen, pulling up an app. "So here's the definition: An outcast. A person despised. That is *moi*, my friend, the ultimate deplorable. And everything I spent a life building ain't worth a steaming pile of shit."

He cast another glance to the end of the bar. The two women now stared at him, while whispering between themselves. Well, let them talk. Everyone else had. "So here's to a career down the tubes, along with everything else, Merry fuggin' Christmas." He downed the rest of the whiskey in a single gulp.

He stared at the counter, rapping his knuckles against the surface. "So how about you, Bernie? You got a happy life? Wife and kids? Girlfriend? Boyfriend? You don't strike me as the cheatin' kind."

"Happy enough."
"I figured. Good, upstanding character, probably never screwed anyone over, faithful to a T. That's the kind of morality that gets you a good job behind a bar, listening to a drunken ass who's just hit rock bottom. Keep up the good work." He set the glass down on the counter as an exclamation point. He'd be winning no points for friendship here, nor did he care.

A voice came from behind. "Excuse me?"

He turned to face the two women from the end of the bar, now standing before him. He looked them over from head to foot, admiring the curves, the lush lips, the silken hair, the whole package times two. Given some other time, he might have made a move. Even tried for a *ménage à trios*. Not now.

The taller one, with medium brown hair hanging past her shoulders, stared at him with an unreadable expression. She still held her glass of red wine in hand. "Excuse me, but aren't you Tony Whitman?"

He studied her for a long moment before answering. "Guilty as charged, my dear."

Her hand snapped in an instant. The contents of her glass crossed the distance, exploding across his face, deep red staining his white shirt. He jerked back. Without a missing a beat, she set her glass alongside him on the bar. "You're a pig. I hope you rot in jail." She turned and marched toward the exit.

Her friend, shorter, blonder, remained long enough to add, "Me too." Then she stomped out the door.

Tony watched her leave. A drop of wine fell from his nose. He reached for the nearby napkin dispenser, pulled a clump out, and dabbed at his face and shirt. No way would the stain come out, not with that amount. "See what I mean?" he mumbled, then pushed his glass toward Bernie. "How 'bout another one. I need it."

The bartender shook his head. "Sorry, sir, but there's no more."

"Course not. I expected that. The perfect kicker to the perfect day."

"You should go to bed, sir. You'll feel better in the morning."

Tony eased himself from the stool to unsteady feet. "I doubt that very much." With a wobbly turn, he exited the bar. Across the hotel lobby. Past the front desk with a lovely receptionist, brunette. Past the nearby unattended concierge desk. Past the massive Christmas tree, with its twinkly lights and promise of peace, good will toward men. Finally, the banks of elevators, with floor-to-ceiling glass walls that looked out to the atrium, decked out in festive decor.

He pressed the button and waited, allowing the moments to tick by, feeling the cold dampness of the wine-soaked shirt against his chest. Feeling the anger build. *How dare the bitch?* She didn't even know him, only hearsay—but that's the down side of fame.

The doors opened and he stepped inside, pressing the button for thirty-two. As the elevator began its ascent, he stared through the glass at the changing perspective of the lobby, growing ever smaller. The upward motion slowed. With a soft ding, the doors opened to his floor.

How had it all come to this, living out of a suitcase, and a brilliant career now apparently over Hotels were nothing new. He'd stayed in the best across the globe, more often than not with a changing roster of sexy bedmates. Some he managed to turn into stars. Most he forgot soon after, but that was a perk of the job. He made certain of that—before his life imploded.

He stepped from the elevator, but after a few yards, he paused and drew himself closer to the ledge looking over the atrium. Visually, the architecture conveyed a stunning design, especially from the height. Angles and curved railing lines shrunk with the distance, reaching the marble floor thirty-two floors below. A wave of vertigo swept over him. He clutched the railing tightly until it passed. How long did it take for him to ride from there to here, forty-five seconds, a minute? How long would the return trip take on a direct route? He lost himself in the calculations, a matter of feet per second applied to the distance, aware that in the grand scheme of things, it served as a simple solution. Quick and easy, for one not ready to pay the piper.

He didn't notice the man beside him until the fellow spoke. "It's quite a view."

Tony said nothing, only acknowledged the other's presence with a grunt.

"A lot of floors, a lot of people," the man added, then allowed silence to fill the gap. He wore his perfect posture as a fashion statement, one hand placed over the other against his solid white suit.

Who the hell wears all white anymore? Tony thought. In an earlier time, the man could be selling ice cream and sodas at a drugstore fountain. He decided not to encourage the stranger with conversation.

It made no difference. "Funny thing, hotels," the man said, "sort of like a weigh station for the masses. Lives pass by, sometimes intersecting, sometimes not. But even the slightest chance encounter can have ramifications to change a life. And here it is playing out before us. Is this mere happenstance, or is there a higher order to things? Fate, perhaps?"

Tony stared at the man. "Do I know you?"

"No, I don't think so." The man grinned, one full of warmth mixed with a mystery. "But I, on the other hand, know you quite well."

"You and everyone else. Not my preference."

"But you're practically household name. Anthony Joel Whitman. Famous director of the Broadway stage, acclaimed writer, numerous awards including five Tonys. Must be a thrill to pretend an award's named after you. Rich beyond measure. Wife... well, wives. Kids." The man raised his eyebrow, like a wink in reverse. "And then, of course, there are all the other women and their... allegations. But you called them out as liars, didn't you?"

Tony felt the irritation building. "Who the hell are you?"

"Why, haven't you guessed?" The man cocked his head. "I'm your guardian angel."

"So you're a lawyer. Seizing on a prime opportunity? I already got one, a damned good one." If a reply could sneer, Tony's stole the show.

The man brushed off the attitude. "Seriously. I am your personal guardian angel. I've been with you your entire life."

"Sure. So where are your fuggin' wings?"

"Wouldn't do well for me to parade through the hotel with them flapping about, would it?"

Tony shook his head, trying to figure a way out of the conversation. "Of course not."

"We have a lot to talk about, Tony. Your past. Present. Future. And you have plenty of free time now. So how will you spend it?"

"What's it to you, buddy?" He paused, then sighed through clenched teeth. "That's right. You're my wingless guardian angel." Caustic laughter spilled, enhanced by the alcohol. "So this is like *It's a Wonderful Life*? You going to tell me how my life was so great, how it changed all the people around me?"

The man's expression turned somber. "No. Not so wonderful. The sad truth is that many people would have been better off without you in their lives. You caused some serious damage over the years. And now you have to figure out what to do about it."

The words did little to quell the incoming storm. Tony stared at the man for some seconds. With everything he had to deal with, the last thing he needed was some self-righteous prick selling him a morality clause.

That's bull. You don't have a clue to my life. And for the record, I've brought joy to a lot of people. I've built careers. Made investors wealthy. Donated to charities. Lots of charity. I can go down the list."

"I don't discount any of that. But you are avoiding the point."

"Which is?"

"You're not a nice person. You hurt the people around you, business associates, friends, strangers... family. Everything you've done is motivated by self-interest. I can go down a list as well, if you want specifics."

Tony clenched his fist, restraining an urge to throw the man against the wall. He took a breath, then another. "You got a name?"

"Why don't you call me Jamie? It's a good, unisex name. I don't want to play favorites."

"That's not funny."

"What's wrong?" After a moment, the man's eyes widened. "Of course. The same name as the plaintiff in your..."

"Enough!" Tony erupted. "You've had your little joke. Now get to the point or get lost."

The man leaned against the railing, arms crossed, with a knowing smile. "You'd like that, wouldn't you? For me to just walk away, as if everything is hunky dory. But it's not that simple. Why, just a few minutes ago, you were looking over this ledge, considering something very drastic. Very permanent. That's why I'm here—because sometimes you have to take that leap of faith to make things better. *Capisce?*"

Tony rubbed his fingers against his brow, as if it might wipe away his troubles. "I'm not in the best of moods, ya know. And kinda drunk."

Jamie put on a comforting face. "I understand. Especially with Ellie walking out on you today after, what, nineteen years?"

"Twenty. She reminded me it was our emerald anniversary."

"And for what it's worth, she was faithful all that time, even though she had numerous opportunities to stray. Remember that producer you worked with some years back? Robert Ellstree, I believe?"

"Eldrich," Tony corrected.

"Right. You nearly lost her that time. He was nuts over her, and would have treated her like a queen. Meanwhile, you've managed to seduce every girl that caught your eye, whether they wanted to or not. Mostly not. And the ones that said 'No?' Well, their careers always seemed to suffer setbacks after, didn't they?

Either way, some took it rather hard. Which is why they're all coming out of the woodwork now—together. They smell blood."

"I didn't want Ellie to go." Tony closed his eyes, a fresh stab from recent events shooting through.

"Not enough... otherwise you might have acted differently." Jamie paused, letting the words sink in. "There's someone I want you to meet."

Tony opened his eyes to find a young woman standing alongside them, so quiet, he hadn't heard her approach. She might as easily have appeared from nowhere. Youngish, perhaps mid-twenties, with long, dark hair hanging to ample breasts. Shapely hips. Full lips. Dark, rich eyes, but set to a pale face, and an expression void of cheer. Something about her seemed vaguely familiar. Out of habit, he immediately undressed her in his mind, liked what he saw.

"Let me reacquaint you." Jamie gestured to the girl. "This is Melanie."

Tony extended his hand. She did not reciprocate, only stared at him. He shifted uncomfortably. "What do you mean, reacquaint? I've never met her before."

The girl shot a look to Jamie. "I told you he wouldn't remember."

Jamie kept a pleasant demeanor. "Memory's a funny thing. Sometimes it requires a trigger, especially when there's been so many. Let's go eight years back, give or take a few months. Revival production of *The Pajama Game*, a suitable title if there ever was one. Melanie was a young hopeful, vying for a role. After the audition, you invited her up to your apartment. When she arrived, you were still in your robe after a shower. Yes, I know you've pulled that stunt many times. Usually it worked. You made advances. She declined. You had her anyway."

Her eyes turned three shades darker. "Then nothing. No call the next morning. No flowers. No role."

"Sorry," Tony muttered.

"And that's all I get now. A half-assed apology. By the way, you're a lousy fuck."

Tony found an ounce of his former bravado. "Whatever. And if you didn't get the role that means you weren't good enough."

Dark eyes turned red. "Just good enough to rape? Is that it? I'm better in bed than on the stage?" She turned to Jamie. "Although we never made it to the bed. He attacked me right there on the floor."

Tony ignored the accusation, scratched at his ear. "Well, I did hope for the best for you. Actors are resilient. How have you gotten along since then?"

She gave another look to Jamie and he nodded. She held her hands up, palms facing Tony. Clearly visible on both wrists were the tracks of red, still oozing where they once gushed. He felt a shudder at the growing comprehension.

"I should have explained," said Jamie. "Melanie's dead. Has been for going on... five years?"

"And four months," she added.

"It's so hard keeping up with time. Such a human concept. Anyway, Melanie had one bad experience after another. The night with you left a lasting wound. Finally, she decided to check out—rather like what you were considering."

Melanie managed a grim smile. "And my last thought was joy—that I'd never have to see or think of you again. Imagine my surprise." She elbowed Jamie. "Like I said before, he's the scorpion, not the frog."

Tony wished for another drink, if only to try to wash the experience away. "You lost me. What scorpion?"

After a comforting tap on Melanie's shoulder, Jamie replied. "Surely you know the fable. The scorpion asks a frog to carry him across the river, but the frog refuses, knowing he'll be stung. The scorpion argues that if he did so, they would both drown. The frog agrees. Halfway across, he stings the frog, and as they drown, the frog asks why. The scorpion answers, 'It's in my nature.' So here's the question: in your life, with its many rivers and many frogs, what will you do now to make amends?"

The inner fire erupted. Tony had never been one to back down from a fight, never retreat. "I don't need to make amends. I plan to fight every charge, deny any wrongdoing." He turned his attention to the girl. "And I refuse to accept any guilt in what you did to yourself—assuming that's what actually happened. All this means is that you're weak and can't handle the real world."

Melanie rolled her eyes, as if not surprised at his outburst. "Can I go now?" she asked Jamie.

"Yes, I'll take it from here. Thanks."

In an instant, she disappeared, the vanishing as surreal as her appearance. Tony looked around him. "How did... where?"

Jamie appeared unfazed. "Humility's a virtue. You might try it."

"I've never needed it before. I got where I am today by determination, and to hell with anyone in my way."

"And where exactly are you now on the success ladder? It doesn't look like the top—rather the opposite."

For once, the snappy retorts Tony excelled in failed to come. Jamie tugged on his shirt, straightening a wrinkle. "Melanie had a rough life, well before you showed up. She didn't have to die the way she chose. There were alternatives that required courage, but she decided not to take a leap of faith. Only after did she see the big picture, but by then, it was too late. We all reach these crossroads sooner or later. Now, it looks as if you have hit yours." He took a step closer. "Things are about to get really nasty for you, between the lawsuits and lawyer fees, divorce, expulsion. What do you do now?"

"They didn't mean anything," he muttered, more to convince himself.

"Perhaps not to you. For others, it was a big deal. Do you have any idea how many women you've slept with over the years, not counting Ellie or your previous two wives? How many random grabs, fondles, insinuations, and inappropriate remarks? Do you have any understanding of the effect it's had? You've left some sizable scars. Do you remember Jeri, the underage girl in New York, eleven years ago?"

"I've never..."

Jamie cut him off. "Yes you did, but probably didn't realize she was only sixteen at the time, not that it would have mattered. You were pretty wasted that night."

Tony looked to the floor, and noticed how his shirt, still red from the wine, had dried to a clammy dampness. In the midst of this intervention, he'd forgotten about it. The stain reinforced his awareness of current problems. "I take it you have a way to make things right?"

"Not really," Jamie laughed. "This is one time where you can't slip a wad of bills on the sly and make your problems go away." He paused, allowing for moment to sink in. "You've dug yourself a hell of a deep ditch, and I don't think any amount of clawing will pull you out completely. However, hope springs eternal when it comes to redemption. Anything might help."

"Like What? Donate more money? Do charity work at a women's shelter? Apologize?"

"At this point, *sorry* only goes so far. It didn't fare well with Melanie. And I don't think a shelter would want you right now."

"That girl saw me as an insect."

"An arachnid, to be precise, but she's got a point. So ask yourself, 'What am I?'" Jamie held up his arm, checking his wrist watch. "Well, Tony, I must be going. I still have other people to see—but I've enjoyed our little chat."

"What? You drop this crap on me, then bail? You said you're *my* guardian angel."

"I am. But even angels can only do so much. After that, it's up to the individual. This is all your doing, not mine."

At once, Tony felt light headed, his legs ready to give, and he reached for the nearby ledge, needing support. "I need to sit." A quick glance around him confirmed the absence of chairs.

Jamie gestured to the carpet, with its decorative motif of maroon swirls. "Make yourself comfortable."

Tony lowered himself to the floor and grounded himself, arms cradled around his legs as a security blanket. "I've no one left to talk to, except my lawyer—who loves me based on dollar per hour."

Jamie joined him on the floor. "You should choose your friends wisely, and hold them dear, the same as your family. Good ones are hard to come by, and you've run through the lot."

"So what you're basically saying is I'm screwed? Is that it?"

Jamie looked to the heavens, considering. "Pretty much. Sorry not to have better news but you reap what you sow. What you do from here is your decision."

"Got any more surprises?" Sarcasm dripped from the question.

"Life is full of surprises, especially for one as busy as you. For example..." With a wave of his hands, much like a master magician, Jamie conjured a bank of fog in front of them, roughly a six-foot square shape. It hovered mid-air like a portal to another realm. In the mist, a figure appeared, manifesting to a female form. "Another one of your transgressions. The girl before you is Sarah. She's nineteen years old and lives in Oklahoma City."

Tony shook his head. "Don't try to pin that on me. I've never been to Oklahoma."

"True. You two have never met, but there is a connection. Sarah is your daughter."

"I don't have a daughter," Tony growled.

"On the contrary. Her mother's name is Constance. You knew her as Connie, but probably paid no attention to her name. She was one of your one-night hotel conquests, this time in New York. Sarah arrived nine months later."

A quality in the girl's features— the jaw structure, the shape of the eyes—caused Tony to pause. He saw the similarities, passed down a generation, and needed no further convincing. "Does she... know about me?"

"Nope. By the time she was born, Connie found a husband. Best to bring a child into the world with a proper family. Unfortunately, he was not good father material." Jamie got to his feet. "Sarah suffered abuse, whenever mom wasn't around. Lost her virginity at twelve. Funny how the wheel keeps rolling, isn't it? But I wouldn't worry about her too much. She's grown into a pretty strong, determined young woman. You might even be proud. As to the dad, well, his time is coming."

Words came with difficulty. "I... didn't know."

"Of course you didn't. Constance was simply a quickie to pass the time. She had plans for her life, but those got scrapped with the child."

"I could have... I guess... helped somehow if I'd known."

"You could have." Jamie looked at the girl in the fog. "But would you? More likely, you would have passed Connie off as an opportunist."

"You don't know that."

"Don't I?" Jamie smiled. "What would a scorpion have done? Consider the whole of your life until now." With a snap of his fingers, the image within the fog shifted, and Tony stared at what first appeared to be an explicit porn film. Then he recognized himself, clawing at Melanie on the floor, while she repeatedly told him to stop. He paid no mind and thrust himself in.

The image changed to Tony, much younger, perhaps high school, acting the bully to a younger boy. He pushed and laughed as the kid fell to the ground. The mist shifted to another scene, Tony shouting at an actress when she failed to deliver to his expectations—a norm for him when directing. Flecks of spit hit her face. She moved to wipe it. "Pay attention to me!" he yelled. Before the image changed Tony saw the tears streaming down her face.

The foggy screen became a slide show of his past, each image held just long enough for Tony to recognize the events. College. The frat party and the girl who passed out after too much alcohol. An easy lay. The two simultaneous girlfriends who didn't know about the other. He had that going for a while. Childhood, rummaging through his father's issues of girly magazines. Wacking off behind locked doors. Copping a feel behind the curtains at an awards ceremony. Getting his face slapped. Good. That meant the babe had spunk. Promises of roles for extra attention and rehearsals under the sheets. Crass remarks, regardless of gender or race. Special disgust leveled at queers. More women. Sex in hotel rooms. Sex in the shower. Blow jobs in the limo. Somewhere in the midst were his wives. Patsy. Helen. Ellie. Moments of affection, and ones filled with hate. Ellie. That hurt the most. Then back to yet another nameless girl, more of them than he ever realized. The pictures flashed by so fast, he could no longer recognize one from the rest. He thought he saw Connie, or someone like her—he'd always had a thing for blondes.

Then, abruptly, the roller coaster ended. Tony had no words, only stared into the murky depths before him. After a long moment, he looked up for some explanation.

Jamie sighed. "Show's over, but you get the general idea. You've got a lot to think about."

Tony shook his head. "You're not being fair."

"What's fair? And for whom?"

"Me. Where's your compassion?"

In response, Jamie knelt, locking eyes. "This..." He rested his hand on Tony's shoulder. "This is compassion. More than that—an opportunity. You know all about opportunities, right? You've had a lifetime of them."

At once, Tony felt his conscience collide with the impassive side he'd spend a lifetime honing. This played out like a master script, exactly as he might have staged it, culminating in a perfect moment of the emotional arc. The sudden revelation. The transition for the final act. Except he had written himself into the storyline with no clear ending—the ultimate writer's block.

Jamie stood and gave another glance at his watch. Shook his wrist, as if checking to see that it worked. Held it to his ear. "I must be going now. Sorry to rush, but that's the life of an angel." With a gesture of his hand, the fog diminished into nothing.

Tony pointed to the watch. "I thought you didn't pay attention to time?"

"It's one of my little indulgences. Helps to remind me of what I once was." Jamie extended his hand, gave Tony's a shake. Solid. Firm. Comforting. "Good luck, Tony. Treat people better. Do good things. I'll be watching you."

With that, Jamie simply wasn't there. Tony stared at a void in space where moments earlier a person, a—something—stood. All at once, he felt more alone than ever before.

He remained sitting, clutching his legs close to his chest, rocking from one side to the other. As much as he desired to discount the last hour, he knew that this had been no hallucination. Even if it had, the substance of the encounter was real. He knew his past, had lived it, and remembered far more than he ever let on. He might deny his doings to the press, the public, the world at large. Putting up a good front came easy. But denial failed when looking inward.

With a sigh, he rose and stepped to the railing. He gazed across the atrium to the other side, floors of rooms set above another. Inside those rooms, lives played out. He watched a couple, the same man and woman he saw earlier in the bar, strolling along the corridor two floors below his. They walked hand in hand, deep into a conversation no one else could hear. She slipped her hand around his waist. He returned the gesture. They opened the door to a room and walked through together. Consensually.

Down below, occasional figures moved across the lobby floor as ants. Who could say from this height if any of them might have a lasting impact on another? The sounds from the atrium wafted upward, echoing against hard surfaces into a muffled combination, further proof of life in flux. What was he other than one more voice in a greater mix? Somewhere above him, the elevator made a stop. A bell dinged.

Jamie spoke of faith, choices, and how they might make a difference. Tony had a lifetime to unravel, with its many intrusions and abuses. Okay, perhaps he had crossed the line on occasion—but surely there were some good deeds too? His life could not be that wrong. He'd been a good husband and provider, father to his children. Excellent at his craft. Tyrannical at times, yes, but it reaped rewards for all involved. The lucky ones made names for themselves, launched careers. So what if he took liberties? He deserved it all.

Still...

He thought of the girl's accusation, and that damned fable. She might as well have held up a mirror for him to see. He knew himself better than anyone else, his strengths and shortcomings, and where his future might lead. He'd directed his life based on his own preferences, giving only when he felt inclined. It had been a wonderful life, until now.

Even if no more allegations were leveled against him, his career was over. Media recognizes a good, juicy story, and struck gold in parading the sordid details of his life for all the world to see. The rest fell as dominoes. In the court of public opinion, he'd already been sentenced. Stick a fork in. He was done.

Too bad, really. He knew the ins and outs of the theater better than anyone, paid his dues early on, and knew his own importance. Even a month earlier, when he spoke, the industry stopped to listen. Now it had turned its back on him. How was that for gratitude?

So, too, his marriage. "I can't pretend any longer," Ellie said before she walked. "God knows I've tried. But I'm not one of your productions, where everything's fine in the final act." Once, love radiated from her face. Now she wore bitterness from too many experiences.

Tony saw what lay ahead. Despite the bravado, he also knew his inner yellow streak, the one he never shared. Always in control, always—and as any good director knows, it's best to let the curtain fall at the right time.

He took off his shoes, one after the other, feeling the softness of the carpet through his socks. He set the shoes against the wall, perfectly aligned ninety degrees. He'd always had an eye for detail.

Then, without further thought, he climbed over the ledge, fully aware of his own nature, and committed to making a leap of faith.

About the Author

David Welling is a Houston-based writer, artist, and graphic designer. His lifelong interest in movies (and the places that show them) led to the writing of *Cinema Houston: From Nickelodeon to Megaplex*, which chronicles the history of movie theatres in Texas' largest city. *Cinema Houston* is the recipient of the 2008 Julia Ideson Award from the Friends of the Texas Room, and the Society of Architectural Historians' 2009 Antoinette Forrester Downing Award. He now writes fiction.

His website and blog is davidwelling.com.

Let the Grapes Grow

By Janet Shawgo

Let the Grapes Grow

THE SOIL IS RICH AND calls for new life to come.

It was the end of the war in Vietnam. The men and women that went to war returned changed or not at all. If you lived in a small Texas town your choices were to work the fields or local factory. It was possible to work in the big cities like Dallas or Houston. James Boyd wanted a college degree. His grades were average, not high enough to obtain a scholarship. James knew his father could not afford to send him to college. He would not work endless hours on the farm as his father had done. The day James turned eighteen he drove to the nearest army recruiter and joined.

"Son, why?" John asked that night at dinner.

"Dad, I can't stay and work here," James responded.

"Did you think about what this will do to your mother?" John asked.

James bowed his head, then looked into his mother's eyes filled with tears.

"Boys like you are dying every day. I won't be able to stand it if you don't come back," Maryanne said.

"I'm sorry it's something I have to do," James said.

"When do you leave?" Maryanne asked.

"Two days," James answered.

James watched his mother leave the table and go outside.

"Son, I did my time in the service. It will change you," John said.

"I promise to write and come home when my time is up," James said.

"Finish your dinner. I'll go see to your mother," John said.

Three years later James kept his promise and came back

home. He stood on the front porch. James looked at the old tire swing in the front yard. His childhood memories flooded his mind including his Dad's voice, *"It will change you."* James entered the army as a child and in one year of fighting wished he had never left Texas. James returned home after his discharge to the nicest time of the year. The weather was cool enough to keep the bugs at bay and allowed a peaceful rest under God's canopy. He slept outside the first week. James needed to be alone and adjust. His parents would stand and watch each night as he left the house. They never questioned or pushed him to talk. The smell of fresh cut grass filled the air as he lay down in the hammock to sleep. James looked into the Texas sky at the bright stars he had missed while he had been gone. These nights outside had begun to ease him back to the safety of home.

The first month was filled with family reunions. It appeared everyone wanted to see James and involve him in the community. James tended to take long walks alone. He needed to decide which direction his life should go. One afternoon he read an article in a co-op magazine about Texas vineyards. The thought he might be able to grow and produce wine appealed to James.

"Dad, could you come outside with me? I have something to ask you," James asked one evening.

James and John walked outside and sat on the steps of the porch.

"What's on your mind son?" John asked.

"I read an article on Texas vineyards. It sounds like something I might be interested in doing," James said.

"Hard work, with no guarantee that you'll grow enough to produce anything," John said.

"I'd like to try," James said.

His father sat for a moment.

"James, old man Grimes has a small vineyard out in Alvord. I heard he needs help. If this is something that you want to do I suggest you spend some time with him. I'll call him in the morning. We can drive over after dinner tomorrow."

The Offer

The next evening James and John drove over to Mr. Grime's

vineyard. James remembered Mr. Grimes being old when he was twelve. The view as they entered the vineyard only heightened and excited James's senses. The rows and rows of twisted vines, green leaves and large clusters of purple grapes, imprinted on James what might be achieved with hard work. When they reached the house, a door opened and a young woman in jeans, and Dallas Cowboy t-shirt, walked outside and waved.

"Who's that?" James asked.

"Carrie Lynn, his granddaughter. She took a year off from college to come help," John said.

"I thought you said he had a small vineyard. This doesn't look small," James said.

"Compared to others in the state, it's on the small side. Grimes told me his harvest this year was going to be one of his biggest. It was too much work for just him and Carrie," John said.

James and John exited the pick up and walked up to the house.

"Evening, John. How's Maryanne?" Carrie asked.

James didn't speak. John turned and looked at his son and smiled.

"Evening, Carrie Lynn. Maryanne is good and sends her regards. Where's your grandpa?" John asked.

"He'll be in shortly. Ya'll want to come in and have something to drink?" she asked.

"That'd be nice," John said.

Carrie looked at James then to John.

"Does he speak?" she asked.

"Eventually," John said.

The three of them entered the house. James watched as Carrie pulled three beers from the fridge. Her brown hair and eyes were beautiful. She walked up to him and held out a bottle.

"John, I thought you said he could talk," Carrie teased.

"I'm sorry, thank you," James said.

She smiled. "He does talk."

The door opened and old man Grimes walked inside. He was taller than James remembered; he was in overalls, work boots and wore a John Deer baseball cap. His father walked over, and shook hands, James followed suit.

"Evening John, James," Grimes said.

"Evening sir," James said.

"Sir?" Grimes looked at James for a moment. "John looks like your boy grew up fine. If you are gonna work for me you can call me Grimes."

"Yes sir," James said.

Grimes walked over to the fridge and pulled out a beer.

"Let's talk business out on the porch," Grimes said.

The three of them went outside. James stood for a moment and took in the evening air. A moment later Carrie walked past him with a rifle. She stood, aimed and fired, killing the large rattler at the end of the porch.

"They're bad out here at times. You ever kill anything?" Carrie asked.

"Carrie Lynn, I think the boy can handle himself. He spent three years in Vietnam," Grimes said.

Carrie immediately regretted her comment. "I'm sorry."

"Its fine, been a while since I've been around rattlers," James said.

"Let's get to it," Grimes told them.

The four sat down in different colored metal chairs that squeaked with their weight.

"James thinks he might want to grow grapes," John said.

"Son, we start work here at sun up and work until dark most days. I'll pay you a fair wage, offer you a place here, and give you what knowledge I have to help you make a decision," Grimes said.

"Thank you," James said.

"Don't thank me yet. I expect a days' work. Carrie is your boss and don't think for one minute she'll go easy on ya. At the end of the season you'll know if this is the type of work fit for you," Grimes said.

"When do I start?

The Process

James arrived the next morning with his clothes and moved into a room outside the processing building. Old man Grimes had him come in for breakfast and then turned him over to Carrie. He thought she was beautiful. Carrie would be his boss and deserved his respect.

"Morning James," Carrie said.

"Morning Ma'am," James said.

Carrie turned around with a spatula in her hand.

"I'm your boss, but the name is Carrie. I don't answer to anything else."

James nodded.

"Now two eggs or three?" she asked

"Three will be good," James said.

Ten minutes later Carrie had eggs, bacon, biscuits and gravy on the table with hot coffee steaming in every cup. The three of them sat down.

"James could you say grace this morning?" Carrie asked.

James looked at old man Grimes.

"It's been a bit, but I'll try."

Carrie reached out for James hand. James voice began to shake.

"Lord, thank you for this food, these people and your grace on my life. Amen."

After breakfast, the dishes were put in the dishwasher and we headed out the door. James looked up as Carrie drove around the house in a small truck. In the back were water, tools, a basket of food, and inside the truck were two rifles

"We'll work the fields until noon. I'll teach while we eat," Carrie told him.

"You two head out. I got bank business to do then I'll meet you for lunch." Grimes told them.

The morning Carrie taught James the lay of the vineyard. She explained the system to harvest. This vineyard was almost fifteen years old, and due to the good year in weather and rain this would be the largest harvest to date.

"We harvest all grapes by hand. I need to hire temps for this season," Carrie told him.

"Dad told me you took a year off from your studies to work here. What's your major?" James asked.

"Chemistry."

James was shocked. "What are you going to do when you finish?"

"Make wine of course," Carrie said, and smiled.

"I've got a lot to learn," James said.

"Time is the factor in growing grapes. You must have good land and patience." she told him.

"I've got the time and patience," James said.

"All you need is land. It must be noon, there's Grandpa," Carrie said.

Carrie pulled up next to his pick up.

"Got good news. The bank said yes to the purchase of those ten acres down the road," Grimes told her.

"That's wonderful news. Good thing you hired James. At some point I need to go back and finish school," Carrie said.

James didn't want to think about Carrie going away. He had so much to learn and it seemed she was the person to teach him. The new acreage Grimes purchased would mean he could start from the beginning.

"James, you need to eat boy. There's heavy work this afternoon to be completed. Carrie will be upset if we don't get it done," Grimes told him.

"Sounds good to me," James said and quickly finished his sandwich.

The days were filled with hard work and evenings being tutored by Carrie. The average time from planting to first harvest was three years. Carrie brought him journals, books and magazines to read and study. James educated himself about the dormancy of vines, pruning, bud break and flowering, veraison and harvest. The grapes were harvested in a certain order, then to production, racking and bottling, and finished bottle. James read each night until he could no longer keep his eyes open. The day for the first harvest arrived and James was ready for next part of the process. He stood and observed as Carrie instructed the temps who had arrived to help this season.

"We'll begin this week on the north side," Carrie said.

"In two weeks, the next section will be ready. It'll mean longer hours," Grimes told the men and women.

"James, you'll go with me. The men and women I've hired have worked here and knowledgeable," Carrie told him.

James didn't argue and was happy to spend time with Carrie. He watched how each cluster was taken and followed her instructions. Harvest lasted from August through Halloween. Each night James was exhausted, but the next morning ready to go again. One morning before Thanksgiving Carrie knocked on his door.

"James, I want you to go with me," she said.

"Where're we going?" James asked.

"I held back a small section of vines. They need to be gathered now," Carrie answered

"Won't they be bad?" James asked.

"The weather held a little longer this year so I left them. The grapes should be sweeter. I want to try and make a dessert wine with them," Carrie explained.

James and Carrie harvested the grapes. She would use her knowledge to create a new product for her grandpa and the vineyard.

"Carrie, did Mom invite you and Grimes to Thanksgiving dinner?" James asked.

"She sure did," Carrie answered.

"Are ya'll coming?" James asked.

"James, I would never miss a chance to have a piece of your mother's pecan pie," Carrie said.

James smiled.

Dormancy

The time James had dreaded arrived. The vines were dormant, fermentation process had begun, and Carrie would return to college tomorrow. The mood at dinner seemed somber this evening.

"Grandpa will continue your education while I'm gone," Carrie told him.

"When will you be back?" James asked.

"At least a year. You can move into my room," Carrie told him.

"James, I've been impressed with you son. I'd like to offer you a job here until Carrie comes back. I've got new acreage to plant and could use your help," Grimes told him.

James sat for a moment looking at both of them.

"I'll stay, but I want the option to buy five of the ten acres from you. I'll pay air price on the land. I'll work it for you and see how the vines grow," James told him.

Grimes took his hand and rubbed it across his whiskers.

"Can ya let me sleep on that?"

"Yes, sir," James answered.

James cooked breakfast the next morning for Carrie and Grimes. His mother had taught him to cook as a boy. She told him a woman liked a man that could do more than bring home a pay check. The smell of pancakes and sausage brought the others to the table. James had made a special peach syrup and melted the butter.

"Good morning!" Carries said.

"Well this is something," Grimes said.

"I wanted it to be a special breakfast for Carrie," James said and dropped his head.

"Breakfast has always been special since you arrived here, James" she said.

Grimes looked at both of them and just shook his head.

After breakfast James washed the dishes and placed everything in its place. He looked up as Carrie brought out two suitcases.

"Time to go," she said.

James picked both of them up and walked outside.

"Carrie Lynn you be careful, call me and say your prayers each night," Grimes said.

"I will grandpa. You watch over James," Carrie said.

"Until you get back, not much I can do for him," Grimes said and laughed.

Carrie walked outside and looked at the sky. "I think it might snow."

James looked at her face. "Tomorrow, not today."

"How can you be so sure?" Carrie asked.

"I've always had a way with the weather. Rain, wind, storms; it saved me more than once in Vietnam," James said.

Carrie walked up and kissed him.

"Grandpa has my number at school, call if you want."

"I'll do that," James said.

Carrie entered the pickup and drove out the gate.

Grimes walked up next to him. "I think you'll be a needing this."

James took the piece of paper with Carries number on it.

"Do you think she would go out with me when she comes

back?" James asked.

"I reckon so son, I reckon so," Grimes said and laughed.

New Life

The next year was difficult for James. His days were long being taught by Grimes about aging, racking and bottling, then finished bottle. The time came when the new fields needed to be worked. James had taken some soil samples to check on what might be needed to improve the growth. He plowed the fields and made trellis. Grimes allowed him to hire a couple of high school boys to help. The weather had not cooperated and a late storm destroyed a section of trellis that had to be replaced. When James didn't have his head buried in books he would steal a moment to call Carrie. As time passed their conversations became less about the vineyard and more on when Carrie would come home. It was the beginning of March.

Grimes drove out to his new fields. He could see James kneeling down.

"James, I've got plants coming tomorrow." he said.

James took the ground in both hands and lifted it to his nose. He stood and turned toward the north.

"I think it'll be good weather for us," James said

"Do you need some help?" Grimes asked.

"I'll make some calls. I know a few teenagers that need gas money," James said and smiled.

"Just get the vines in the ground, can't afford to lose any," Grimes said.

"Not gonna happen," James said.

The vineyard excelled past the previous year in growth and production. Grimes would have another high yield harvest. The new fields had prospered. He looked up as James came into the house.

"You're going to have an early harvest in the north fields this year," James told him.

That means we'll need extra help. I need to start early to hire the help we'll need," Grimes said.

He wished Carrie was back here. The vineyard had grown faster than he could handle. If James wasn't here he would have been in trouble.

"Carrie called last night. She said she might be home before final harvest," James told him.

"Well now that would sure be a big help to me and put a smile on your face," Grimes teased.

"If she can finish her final paper she'll be home," James told him.

Grimes never heard Carrie ever call this place home until James came to stay.

Harvest was bigger than last year. All the regulars came and new ones were hired. James took the responsibility to teach the new hires proper way to harvest so the vines were not damaged. Sun up to dark everyone worked. James was the first person up and the last to go to bed.

Grimes had taken a few moments to check his accounts. He was proud of James and had made the decision to sell him the five acres. He looked up as James entered the house.

"We have a problem," James told him.

"A couple of the workers quit?" Grimes asked.

"No, a storm is coming," James said.

"Rain won't be bad. Everyone will be muddy but..." Grimes said.

"Not rain, snow," James said.

"Too early not possible," Grimes said.

"I'm telling you we've got two days before it comes," James said sternly.

Grimes knew James had been right in the past about the weather. If this was possible he would lose the last half of his harvest. The new vines needed to be covered.

"We need another fifty helpers," Grimes said, then ran his hand through his hair.

"We need a miracle," James said.

Neither James nor Grimes slept much that night. The added workers they needed weren't available due to harvest across the state. James had made a call to Carrie He advised about the weather and potential loss of the harvest. He lay on his back waited for the alarm, when the smell of fresh coffee made him sit up. James met Grimes in the hallway.

"Well that answers my question," Grimes told him.

They walked into the kitchen where Carrie and thirty men and women stood.

"I heard you needed some help, so we brought coffee and donuts. There's not enough time for a regular breakfast I'm told."

James walked over hugged and kissed her. A loud approval was sounded by the added help.

"Who are these people?" James asked.

"These are friends from college, avid wine drinks and just good people," Carrie said.

James hadn't meant for Carrie to leave school but he was glad to see her. The help she brought helped to finish the harvest. The new plants were covered for the storm. The individuals who didn't leave before the storm arrived stayed with members of the community. The unexpected snow storm ruined the harvest for many of the vineyards in the area, except Grimes.

The old men of the town gather at Grimes winery and ponder on how he knew about that storm. He just smiled and said, "Just lucky." Grimes was more than good on his word to let James buy the five acres. He gave James and Carrie the other five for a wedding present the next spring.

"Where's James?" Grimes asked, as he poured a cup of coffee.

"Checking on the new vines," Carrie said.

"Good man you got there," Grimes told her.

"Thanks to you," Carrie said and headed out the door.

Grimes smiled.

James stood and looked at the growth of the vines in just a year. He knelt and felt the earth in his hands. The sound of the pickup made him turn around. His journey had just begun.

"What are you smiling at?" Carrie asked, as she walked up to him.

"Thinking about how lucky I am to be here," James said and wrapped his arms around her.

"Grandpa told me about another ten acres for sale on the other side of the highway," Carrie said.

"We have another year and half before these vines produce. What do you think? Can we do it?" James asked.

"I think we need to do what grandpa has done in the past," she answered.

"What's that?" James asked.

"Plant the vines and let the grapes grow."

About the Author

Janet Shawgo lives in Galveston Texas but over her twenty plus years as a travel nurse her life has crossed the United States.

Being a nurse for over thirty-three years, most of those in labor and delivery, has assisted in her writings. She starting writing in 2009 and has five books published to date.

Her *Look For Me* series has some thirty awards and acknowledgements. Janet has added some interest to her stories from her own travels. Research and actually putting feet on the ground helped to bring my stories to life.

Writing has become important to Janet. She has many stories running through her mind and cannot wait to share them with others.

West Texas Initiative

By Warren B. Smith

West Texas Initiative

"DAN, HE SHOULD BE IN the coffee shop now," said Randall, my supervisor. "There's millions at stake here—we have to find those accounts before he gets out of the country. We're sure he knows we suspect him of scamming our investors. You need to be convincing and make him think we're still early in the audit. Be flexible, there's no telling what kind of con-man act he'll try."

"Yes, sir."

"And make sure the microphone doesn't show, Dan. We need to pull this off without raising suspicion. If he sees it, this whole thing will blow up on us, he'll run, and we'll lose millions"

"The mic's hidden under my lapel Randall and I've tested it to be sure we get a good play-back."

"Good, you know details are the key. This is your big chance, Dan. You have an opportunity to prove yourself as management material. You're five years out of college, so it's time to step up your career. Convince him we're still auditing records of the production company partnerships. You do that and he should be comfortable hanging around a while longer."

"I'm nervous, Randall. I'll do my best, but I have no experience working with slick con-men. No telling who all he and his good ol 'boy cronies have involved in the scam. In order to put pump jacks out there not hooked up to wells, there had to be a lot of people involved. Heck, everybody in town is probably deep in this scam. They've manufactured fake drilling and workover reports on the wells as well as fake records for all the pumping operations. This is big, Randall.

"Aw, grow up, Dan! Take initiative. Show us what you can do. Don't worry. You look like a geek auditor. A little nervousness will fit. Use it. Be yourself. We only need one day. We don't want him to spook and run."

"Yes sir. I'm three blocks away, so I'll hang up now and move up to the coffee shop."

"Relax, Dan, you'll do fine." Randall said and hung up.

I keyed my girlfriend's number into the cell phone and pushed the dial button.

She answered on the first ring. "Are you ready for your big day?" I loved her sexy voice, it fits her personality.

"Yeah, big day for sure. My boss is riding my ass hard—he's always reminding me to 'take initiative.' That SOB thinks I'm focused on nothing but a career opportunity today. I'll take initiative all right."

"You'll get your dream, love. Hang in there. There's a Caribbean island waiting for you!"

"Thank you. I love you, babe, but I gotta' run." I clicked off the line.

I drove the three blocks to the coffee shop, mulling over details in my mind.

Basic accounting sucks. Day after day, crunching numbers, confined to an office cubicle. Not for me! Someday I'll be running a charter business in the islands. One of my friends is managing a yacht charter business in the Virgin Islands. That's the kind of job I'm going to have. A tropical sunset every day, and most of all, peace and serenity.

With this job I have "P&L responsibility." The profitability of the partnerships is on my back. I'm expected to bring more profit to the bottom line. With my promotion I inherited this client so I dug into the records of the oil & gas partnerships in the portfolio. Right off, I found transactions that didn't make sense. I suspected the General Partner was scamming the partnerships, but I needed to prove it. Millions of dollars were at stake. I am expected to get to the bottom of it one way or the other.

The storefront coffee shop was easy to pick out among the dilapidated old buildings on the main street. It was the only building with an open business. I pulled in behind the second of the only two cars in front of the coffee shop.

I reached into my inside jacket pocket and switched on the transmitter. "Hear me OK, Randall?"

"Yeah, loud and clear," he responded. "Let's get on with it, Dan, and don't forget to pull the earpiece."

"Got it." I pulled out the earpiece and disconnected it. I thought about this whole ordeal for a few minutes—strange how things can turn out. Hope I've got all the preparations right and I play a believable part. If I screw this up, the fallout will haunt me the rest of my career, if I have one left, that is.

Hot dusty winds fit the depressing atmosphere of this dying West Texas oil town. I hate the heat. I haven't even opened the car door yet and can already feel the grit from the blowing dust grinding between my teeth.

Squinting against the howling wind and blowing dust, I opened the car door. I pulled my collar tight to block the grit from going down my shirt. It was a wasted effort. At the coffee shop, I opened the outer door and stepped into the vestibule. The inner door handles were made from pipe tongs, a specialized tool found on the floor of a drilling rig. The handle was easy to grab. Ingenious.

I pulled the door open and stepped into the coffee shop. Everything in this dive looked run down and worn out. Slow turning ceiling fans hung from high, dingy ceilings. Worn tables and chairs populated the dining area. The 1950's style black and white checkerboard floor tiles showed decades of use. Ugly wood slat blinds blocked afternoon sun from entering side street windows. Paint peeled from walls and the ceiling. Who in the hell would want to live in this town? Somewhere in this place should be the partnership's operations manager.

All the seats were empty except for the next-to-last booth on the right where I saw a cowboy hat perched atop an old faded blue jean jacket separated by thick brown hair. The man wearing it sat in the booth facing away from the entrance, and that struck me as odd.

A tight-fitting black and white uniform accented the slender body of a young waitress. She leaned against the counter with one hand. Her other hand was hiked up on her hip. He felt her eyes on him admiring his slim athletic physique, blond hair and bright blue eyes. She smiled, winked, and asked "Can I help you? Menu? Coffee? How about some delicious homemade peach cobbler that will go great with coffee." This she said while slowly tucking her long blond hair behind her ear.

She's nice looking with a slim, cute body and a smile to match, but she's young.

"Thank you. I'll have the coffee and pass on the cobbler for now, but—it sounds good. Maybe later."

The hat swiveled around and the old man under it spoke. "Grab your coffee and come
have a seat over here young fella'."

The waitress said "Coffee's coming up," as she sauntered over with a carafe, placed a cup and saucer on the lunch counter and poured the steaming black coffee. "I'm Audrey, let me know if you need anything else, sugar," she said with a wink.

"Thank you, Audrey." I smiled and winked back at her.

I tried to look calm, picked up the coffee and walked over to the booth. I felt the eyes of the waitress boring a hole in my back, but knew Randall was listening to every sound, and would follow the conversations.

The man in the booth stared at me a moment, took a last drag off a burned-down cigarette, and stubbed it out in the ashtray. He blew a cloud of smoke toward the ceiling as he exhaled. He had a weathered face, a gaunt look, and brown hair that was bushy, but neatly trimmed. His skin was ruddy, and deeply weathered. The western style shirt under the open Wrangler denim jacket looked new. His cowboy hat was pristine and perfectly blocked. Although his features were rough, he had a friendly air about him that put me at ease. I could see why he was such a slick con-man.

"I guess you're the man I came to see. I'm Dan Miller, and you must be Buddy Pickins."

He looked at me with a blank expression. "No, I ain't Buddy Pickins."

"Why'd you motion me over? Who are you?"

"Do you need cream and sugar for your coffee?" asked the man in the booth.

"No, I need to meet with Buddy and . . . "

"Buddy's in the morgue."

"In the morgue? What the hell happened?" I tried to sound shocked.

"You might as well calm down and have a seat, young man. You and I are not adversaries here." He drew out a worn leather wallet and opened it to show a badge and ID for the county sheriff's office. "I'm Special Investigator Will Roberts. I'm a retired Texas Ranger working special assignments as an investigator for the county. And you, young man, just walked into a nightmare. Tomorrow the FBI will be questioning everybody that ever knew or talked to Buddy, especially business associates."

"What?" I asked as I slid into the booth.

"Last night Buddy took three bullets in the back. A .357 judging from the exit holes. A lot of people are running scared. Reminds me of Billy Sol Estes, but you're too young to remember that case."

He continued. "The shit hit the fan here this morning and we've been scrambling to find the players before they vanish. A judge in Midland will be issuing subpoenas and warrants tomorrow. Bank accounts, assets and everything related to the partnerships will be locked up tight by late tomorrow morning. I suspect that your company dodged a big-ass bullet if they haven't put any money into Buddy's deal yet.

"He's a slick dude. It looks like he's been taking investors' money for drilling development wells that weren't drilled. Then he charged for the regular workovers to keep 'em pumping, but actually only had half as many to do. Of course the real wells had to pump twice their allowable so that he'd have the correct total volume produced. It was pretty slick, and violated a ton of state and federal laws. He scammed millions by doing it.

"Oh—my—God!" I said, "This could bankrupt the company!"

"If I were you, I'd call your boss tonight and let him know that the whole thing, including your deal, has exploded. You might suggest to your boss that you go on to Midland tomorrow to meet with the investigators. Your company can help put these guys away. I'll give you the contact names and information. A multi-agency task force will meet after lunch tomorrow in Midland to plan on how to proceed."

"How'd you know about this meeting?"

"It was in Buddy's cell phone calendar."

"Damn, I can't believe this disaster! And, it's already five o'clock. If I leave now I can be back in Big Spring by six-thirty or seven, but everybody's gone home for the day. I'll have to call the company president tonight at home and let him know."

"That's a good plan young man. Yeah, I'd like to chew the fat with you too and fill in the details, Dan, but it wouldn't help at this point. We both got work to do, so let's get out of here."

He gave me contact names and numbers and we left the coffee shop. I walked to the rent car, started it up, and pulled onto the street headed south toward Big Spring. After a few blocks I pulled over to the shoulder to call Randall.

"I'm sure he bought it," I said. "Buddy's a damn good con man, had a good cover and played it perfectly. He's ballsy, slick, and likeable, and he knows the jig is up. I'm surprised he even met with me."

"Yeah," Randall responded, "but he had to know how much we knew and to try to throw off our investigation, and possibly buy some time. You did well, Dan, and I heard every word. You should get an Oscar for that one!" He laughed. "You did a convincing job of sounding shocked and worried. He's a real character, but we cannot forget that he's a crook and if he hadn't been so damn greedy, he might have gotten away with it. He could be in the Caymans right now. That was brilliant the way you revised the deal, I think he fell for it hook-line-and- sinker. You out-conned the con-man!"

"Thanks, Randall."

"You sounded good. I'm sure he thinks he snookered you with that act and bought enough time to escape. But I have a surprise waiting for him when his flight arrives in Houston for the connection to Grand Cayman!"

"Are you staying over in Midland tonight, Randall?"

"No I'm confident you can handle it. I'm leaving now to catch my flight out of Midland-Odessa. Give me an update tomorrow afternoon."

We clicked off. And I turned off my microphone. I tossed the company cell phone on the seat as I headed for Big Spring.

I left the parked car and stepped into my room at the Best Western Hotel in Big Spring.

Once inside I pulled out my laptop, hooked up the Ethernet connection, and triggered the power. I connected to the internet and logged onto my accounts. "Fantastic. I see the deposit!"

I picked up the new cell phone from Walmart, sat on the edge of the bed, and dialed the lone number in the directory.

"Did he buy it?" He asked.

"Hook, line, and sinker," I responded.

"If you want to ride with me young fella', you need to be at the Stephens County Airport by 10 PM. We'll be out of US airspace before 8 AM tomorrow."

"Yes Sir. We'll be there."

I hung up the phone, and turned to Audrey who had been rubbing my back. We need to get going before long, sugar. And I'm ready for that peach cobbler," I said with a chuckle.

"Don't worry, Love. I told you Daddy won't stiff you, and he won't leave without us either." She giggled. "Do you want the peach cobbler —now?'

"I lifted her in my arms and carried her toward the bed. Darlin' you know there's something I want right now, and we have an hour before we have to leave."

Audrey kissed me as she unbuttoned the top button of my shirt.

About the Author

Warren B. Smith recently retired from a sales career spanning over 40 years in the oil and gas industry. The new-found free time has given him the opportunity to pursue a life-long dream to write. An avid reader, his goal is to develop the skills to write short stories and eventually a novel. He prefers action-packed stories with a humorous flare. Carl Hiaasen and Janet Evanovich are two of his favorite authors. Warren has a Bachelor of Science degree from Texas A&M University and lives in Houston with his family, which includes three dogs, his wife, three children, two grandchildren, a nice garden, and one dead houseplant that gratefully never needs watering.

Come Saturday Morning
By C. Hart Palumbo

Come Saturday Morning

GWEN SAW HER SISTER'S car parked at the main house. Bright red against the spring green expanse of central Texas pasture that separated her white clapboard ranch-style from the rambling farmhouse they'd grown up in. Nothing else looked quite that red—not even the Indian paintbrush wildflowers. It sent a familiar prickle of mixed emotions along the back of her neck. Relief that someone else stepped up to look after Mama. Excitement that Tish was home. Hurt that her sister hadn't yet made the trip across the three-hundred yards or so. Resentment that she could breeze in for a couple of days, play the heroine, and then go back to her life in Houston. It was always the same.

Funny. These feelings should have faded over the last few months. After the years when Tish came home so rarely it seemed a true event. But since their mother's illness, Tish had made the supreme effort to come home almost every weekend. It was the least she could do. Gwen dealt with it all the rest of the time.

Not that she disliked her sister. On the contrary, she loved her. Truly loved her. She never seemed to take offense to Gwen's 'moods'. She just took it in stride, as she did everything else. It was her most insufferable trait—her calm, easy going competence. Bad manners never ruffled her. Nor ill tempers. In fact, the only thing that ever got to Tish was stupidity. She possessed little patience for that—actually none. It explained why her sister never had kids. Children were by nature stupid. Growing up being a process of becoming less stupid.

Gwen hooked up the garden hose to the sprinkler. She'd better turn it on for a bit this morning before the sun got too high. If she waited, she would get caught up and before she knew it the Texas sun would be pounding down and watering would parboil the roots of her carefully planted vegetable garden. There were claw marks among the delicate Crowder pea plants. Some armadillo no doubt. She pulled a caterpillar off a tomato plant and flicked it hard on the ground. "Damn. Got to get that bug spray when I go to the store."

Walking around to the back of the house, she attacked the pile of wet laundry in the basket she'd left just outside the sliding glass door. The morning air glistened, beautifully clear and painfully blue. The breeze made a soft sighing sound through the pecan trees.

Gwen especially loved the early mornings, when everyone else slept and the day still belonged to her. On days like this, she really didn't mind that her clothes dryer was on the fritz. She enjoyed hanging the fresh laundry on the clothes line. The mechanical task took only a tiny part of her mind. She could daydream with the rest. Something she'd always enjoyed. But lately, she hadn't found much time.

The smell of damp lemon verbena assailed her. She needed to remember to cut off the sprinkler when she finished with the laundry.

The damp shirt in her hands gave off a fresh Tide smell—even though she didn't use Tide anymore. She bought the soap she had a coupon for or whatever was on sale. But she still associated the smell with Tide, because her mother had always used it. The cool damp heaviness of each garment as she picked it up seemed somehow reassuring. Normal.

She pinned them carefully to the line, as Tish had taught her when they were children. *Funny! I haven't thought of that in ages.* Closing her eyes and holding the shirt to her face, she could almost remember what it felt like to stand on a metal lawn chair and take a heavy damp towel from her sister's hands. Tish always popped it in the breeze with a loud crack. Her body remembered balancing on the precarious edge of the chair and leaning almost beyond her reach to clamp the second pin on the corner—the relief when she recovered her balance. She could almost feel what it was like to be small and light—almost.

Unconsciously, she snapped the garment. She took one of the clothes pins attached to the broad expanse of her shirtfront and jammed it in place. *I better get cracking.* The baby would wake up before long and everything would speed up. Keeping an eye on a three-year-old and getting anything accomplished was almost impossible. Toby would get up eventually and expect breakfast.

It would have been easier if Chris were coming. But her oldest daughter cancelled her scheduled visit at the last minute. When she first chose to live with her father, Chris came home almost every weekend. But lately, her visits had become more and more rare. Gwen had primary custody and knew she could insist. But Chris was thirteen now, a teenager. Only natural that she thought of better things to do. She took after her Aunt Tish in that way.

The willow basket was empty. Bending over to catch the handle, she felt a twinge in her lumbar. The car accident left her with a weak back. Since Mary's birth, the pains had grown progressively worse. She tried to be careful picking things up, especially the baby. But there was no getting around the real cause.

At over two-hundred pounds, she wore a 44 DDD. It would be interesting to weigh each breast and see exactly how much of her weight she carried up front. Fifty pounds maybe? Twenty-five each?

She tried to walk with the willow basket on her head, like those women in National Geographic. It wasn't that hard. Actually, it might be easier if the basket was full. It would balance better.

"Hey, Lady? You practicing for the circus?"

The basket tumbled to the ground. Her sister stood framed in the sliding glass door, easily three inches taller and about seventy pounds thinner. Some things in life just weren't fair.

"No, I've been watching too much television. What are you doing up so early?"

"Oh, I woke up about 4:00 and couldn't go back to sleep. I drank some milk, read for a while, but nothing worked. I started to brew coffee for Daddy, but the last time he complained all weekend about non-coffee drinkers using his percolator. You'd think it was some sacred voodoo rite or something." Tish flung her arms loosely around Gwen and gave her a squeeze. "I thought I'd take a chance somebody was awake down here."

Gwen led the way into the house and tossed the basket toward the laundry niche. "Sit down. I was going to put on another wash and start on these dishes before the hungry horde wakes up."

"I'll wash. You dry," Tish offered. Gwen started to protest. She didn't keep rubber gloves. Tish's nails were long and bright orange. Well a little dish-washing never hurt anyone.

"You'll have to run fresh dishwater. They've been soaking all night, so the suds are gone." Gwen turned to a pile of clothes beside the washing machine. She'd do brights next. She could use cold water and leave the hot for the dishes.

Turning back, Tish had already donned an apron and was up to her elbows in rich warm lather. She'd used more detergent than necessary. The drain board was already more than half full. Gwen dug for a fresh dish towel with no holes. They worked side by side for several minutes in easy silence.

"I'm worried about this medicine Mama's taking. It's new. It's not like the old chemo." Tish paused to use the scratch pad on a stubborn spot. "She doesn't get nauseous. But she gets this burning sensation and the only thing that stops it is eating something. Everyone else in the world turns to skin and bones on chemo, and Mama puts on sixty pounds."

"You're exaggerating. She was overweight to start with." Gwen's weight problems were a legacy she shared with her mother. "But, the doctor did say something this last time."

"Well, it's about time. Whenever I ask Mama about it she says if the doctor doesn't care, why should she?" Tish rinsed a soapy plate. "I think she's eating as some sort of consolation for being sick."

Gwen's defenses went up. Obviously this was her fault. "Well, you can't really blame her. She is sick. Very sick. What difference does it make if she gains weight?"

Tish's jaw dropped. "It could make a big difference in her overall health. All this extra body fat is not making the radiation therapy any easier. It's symptomatic of her whole attitude toward this illness."

"What attitude is that?" Gwen asked, all innocence.

"This whole martyred routine. She takes no responsibility for her own recovery. It's like the cancer is something outside of her. It has nothing to do with her. It's up to God and the doctors to deal with it and she's just waiting to see how it turns out."

Gwen flinched. She knew exactly what Tish was talking about. *God, I ought to know!* Gwen spent every day with her mother.

It fell to her to drive her back and forth for the treatments. A hundred and twenty miles round trip. She cleaned her mother's house instead of her own, did the grocery shopping, and listened to her mother cry. She gritted her teeth and took over when things needed to get done. Yes, she knew. But it irked her that her sister had noticed and brought it up, almost as a reproach. "That's kind of harsh don't you think?"

"No, I don't." Tish turned and took the dish towel to wipe suds from her arms. There were tears in her eyes. It had been a long time since she had seen Tish cry over anything but a sad movie. "I'm scared, Gwenny."

Don't do this to me. I can't take it if you fall apart too.

"Not nearly as scared as she is."

"I think that's what scares me the most," Tish said.

Then they hugged, for real this time. Tish held onto the solid mass of her sister as if to a life raft. "You know, Gwenny. All those years when we were growing up and she treated me like an adult, I was her confidante. I saw her in every kind of mood; depressed, happy, angry, spiteful, funny, even self-pitying. But I don't ever remember seeing her afraid. I don't know what to do with that."

Gwen held her sister, and it felt. How ironic? They had switched places in life. Tish had been a grown-up from the time she was born, or so it seemed. Gwen was the carefree prankster, the flirt, the outrageous adventurer. Looking back, it almost seemed like someone else's life. As if it were a movie she saw long time ago and remembered as funny and enjoyable, but the details blurred. In the screenplay of their lives, they switched parts somewhere along the way. She suspected she had become a supporting character in someone else's movie.

Gwen dug out the hot chocolate. It was still early enough to enjoy it. The day might become stifling, but not for an hour or so. They curled up on the sofa, blowing on their mugs and marshmallows, just like when they were kids. Gwen pounded and clumped the sofa cushions into a comfortable nest. They sat close, their bodies touching at various points in an easy way. Gwen grunted slightly as she shifted her position, taking the weight off the pin in her hip, resting her arm and one breast on the pillow.

Tish eyed her. "Mama says your back is bothering you again."

Gwen grimaced. *Leave it to Mama to pass on every bit of information.* No doubt, she also relayed the latest string of arguments with Toby.

Tish set her cup on the coffee table. "Roll over. I'll rub your back."

"Frankly, it's not very comfortable on my stomach." Gwen arranged the pillows to create a hollow for her breasts. It took some doing. Finally, she found a comfortable position.

Pushing the shirt up out of the way, Tish said, "When are you going to get those things downsized? That's your back problem."

"Duh, you think?"

Tish laughed at Gwen's imitation of her teenage daughter.

"When did you arrive at that astonishing hypothesis?"

"You know a doctor would recommend the surgery for your health. Insurance should cover it. Don't you guys have insurance, yet?"

"No. Toby never stays on a job long enough." She felt Tish's fingers dig in. "Don't say it."

"I wasn't going to say anything," Tish said. She continued to work the muscles in the small of Gwen's back.

Maybe she'll let it go.

"I can't help but think that you and the baby could get along just as well without Toby."

The truth of the statement didn't lessen the hurt. The few times they'd split for a few weeks, Gwen managed to pay the bills with her various part-time jobs. She actually saved a little. But Toby always got in over his head and begged to come back. And she always let him. She wasn't sure why.

"I'm really enjoying this, don't spoil it, okay."

"All right." Tish worked the muscles; pressing on the knots until they loosened and massaging the tendons until they lengthened. Then she unconsciously settled into the old pattern of running her fingertips lightly over the skin, barely scoring the surface with her nails. It was closer to tickling than anything. She had done it for hours after Gwen's childhood nightmares. It soothed them both.

"What happened to your plans to go to interior design school, Gwenny? I thought you really wanted to do that."

She had. More than anything she ever wanted. But she had only Chris to worry about then. She'd planned it all out. Bill agreed to take Chris for a year, maybe two, while she went to school in Austin. She could live cheap if she didn't have to support her daughter. No one pinched a penny closer than she did. She got the brochures, applied for a student loan. Everything seemed set, but there was the small matter of an entrance exam. She was never good at tests in school and she failed the math portion. It was an omen. Shortly after that, she discovered she was pregnant with Mary. That put an end to it.

"I got married. I couldn't take care of a baby and go to school." She rolled over and sat up.

"Other people do. You could come and stay with me." Tish got up on her knees, a look of eager excitement on her face. "You could bring the baby and move in with me. I've got a spare bedroom. You could do it, I know you could."

For a moment Gwen's heart fluttered with something like hope, even excitement. But it flickered and went out. The heaviness descended again. The oppressive weight that seemed almost to suffocate her some days. "Nah, it was a silly dream. Whose house would I decorate here in the country?"

"You could come and stay with me, you know. I would love that. Really." A strange look came over Tish's face.

She's lonely. It occurred to Gwen that her perfect sister, with the perfect life might not be happy. But then it passed.

"No. I don't want to raise Mary in a city. I want her to have a childhood like we had."

"Really?" There was an edge to Tish's voice.

They looked away from each other, remembering the bitter quarrels between their parents, their father's drunken binges, their mother's constant harping. Each of them put the memories away before the other could see it on her face.

"Yeah, I guess you're right." Tish got up and brushed the wrinkles from her neat khaki trousers. "I better get back to the house before Mama wakes up. She had a lot of pain last night. I made her listen to the CDs I brought. She stopped crying after a while and went to sleep." She smiled her perfect practiced smile. "You guys come on down to the house later. I'll make lunch."

"We'll see. I really need to clean the house while I have the chance."

"Okay, well, if you change your mind, call me."

Tish set off to walk the three-hundred yards across the pasture to her parents' house. But she didn't hurry. The bluebonnets were going to seed, replaced by Indian paintbrush, wild flox, and some yellow flower she couldn't name. Stooping, she picked a purple wine cup from between the milkweeds. It had almost no fragrance.

What ever happened to my prom queen sister, she mused.

She stopped dead in her tracks, remembering something Mama had said recently. "Gwen thinks she lived through that terrible car accident so there would be someone to take care of Daddy and me."

The day seemed suddenly very grey.

About the Author

C. Hart Palumbo was born and raised in central Texas, in a town too small to have a Dairy Queen, which in Texas is pretty darn small. She went to college to become an Art and English major and ended up in Theatre quite by accident.

After graduation she decided to bring the light of art back to Lexington, her hometown. Accepting a job as head of the English department at her old high school, Palumbo was only three years older than her graduating seniors, including her own brother. You should NEVER go back to teach in your own high school.

She left teaching for a few years and moved to Houston, where she worked in professional theatre, helping to grow two mid-sized theaters. After studying at the American Conservatory Theatre in San Francisco, she completed her MFA at the University of Texas at Austin. She has spent twenty plus years of her life as an actor, director and arts administrator in Houston, Austin, Seattle, San Francisco, Los Angeles, and Moscow, Idaho.

These days she can be found as a professional technical writer and instructional designer for the oil and gas and financial industries, but continue to teach theater and film appreciation, direct, act, and work with playwrights to 'fix' their plays. Currently focused on becoming a published novelist, she has written a contemporary romantic mystery in the cozy vein and a literary coming-of-age novel set in rural Texas in 1965, the year Texas schools desegregated. She is a proud union member of Actors Equity and SAG/AFTRA, and belong to Mystery Writers of America (MWA), Society for Children's Book Writers and Illustrators (SCBWI), Houston Writer's House (HWH), and Houston Writer's Guild (HWG), as well as two critique groups. She currently resides in Houston with her two cats.

The Yellow Rose
By Janet Shawgo

The Yellow Rose

CAITLYN STANDINGS BROWN stood and observed her baby sister, Cierra, try on her wedding gown for a final fitting. She could not believe in two weeks their father would walk Cierra down the aisle at the community church in Canyon, Texas. A tear ran down the side of Caitlyn's face. She wished Mother was alive to see the wonderful women her four daughters had become. At the age of fifteen Caitlyn became the woman of the house. The responsibility for three younger siblings seemed a burden in the beginning. She refused to disgrace her Mother's memory and did the best she could in the early years. Cierra was two years old when Mother passed. The small child asked for her every night that first year.

"Mommy, Mommy," Cierra cried.

Caitlyn would hold her and rock her to sleep. She hummed the melodies Mother once sang to all of them. The first year was hard for everyone in the house.

The two trouble makers in the family were Cindy, ten, and Cathy twelve. Caitlyn smiled as she remembered the notes and calls from their teachers on grades, attitudes, and any problem that arose. She was sister, Mother and go between when issues escalated to Dad.

"Dad, let me punish them," Caitlyn begged him.

"Not this time. You have enough on your shoulders and it's gone too far," he said.

Those were very unpleasant times for Caitlyn. Cindy and Cathy finally decided her punishment wasn't as severe as Dad's. We worked together, adjusted and promised to keep Mother's memory alive for Cierra.

"Look Cierra this is Mommy," Cindy said, and pointed to

pictures in the album.

"Mommy. Where's Mommy?" Cierra asked.

"Caitlyn, what do I tell her?" Cindy called.

"Tell her the truth. Mommy is in heaven," Caitlyn said.

Death is a difficult subject to discuss at any age. It was several years before Cierra would understand.

Dad asked me to follow him to the attic one cool fall afternoon. We climbed the stairs together to the locked door. He handed me the key.

"Caitlyn it's time," he said.

"What do you want me to do with everything?" Caitlyn asked.

"Keep what you and your sisters want, then take the rest to the church," he said.

Caitlyn watched him turn and go back downstairs. She heard him begin to cry as he reached the bottom step. Caitlyn couldn't imagine how she would ever be able to pick and choose. Any item in this room had a place in their hearts. Dad spent nearly every night up here and stayed for hours. Caitlyn felt this was the place he could be near his wife and grieve. She worried items would be in disarray as it had been three years. Caitlyn opened the door and was shocked at the condition of the attic. It was spotless. The boxes had been stacked and labeled which would make her job easier. Caitlyn walked through to prepare some type of plan when she found her Mother's hope chest.

"Caitlyn one day this will be yours," She could hear her Mother's voice. Caitlyn walked over, knelt down, closed her eyes and opened the chest. The scent of cedar filled her senses. When she opened her eyes, they began to fill with tears, quilts, beautiful quilts. Caitlyn thought back on her Mother's life. She had been a stay at home Mom, belonged to the PTA and active in the church. Caitlyn knew two evenings a week Mother had gone into town.

"Dad, where's Mother going?" Caitlyn asked.

"Mother is going to visit with friends," Dad said.

Caitlyn realized where their Mother had gone, twice a week, every week, until she was no longer physically able to leave the house. She ran down stairs and called Irene's Quilt Shop.

"Hello, is Miss Irene in? Tell her it's Caitlyn Standings," she said.

It seemed forever before she heard a familiar voice.

"I wondered how long it would be before you found them," Irene said.

"May I come and speak to you?" Caitlyn asked, her voice trembled.

"Of course, darling I'll always have time for you," Irene said.

Caitlyn looked at her watch and walked into the family room. Cathy and Cindy were doing homework.

"I need to leave for a while can you two watch Cierra?" Caitlyn asked.

"Where you going?" Cathy asked.

"Miss Irene's quilt shop," Caitlyn said.

"Does Dad know?" Cindy asked.

"No, but he's gone until Monday," Caitlyn answered.

"How long will you be gone?" Cathy asked.

"Just a few hours, it's about Mom," Caitlyn said.

Cindy and Cathy looked up, and nodded in approval. Caitlyn walked out the front door, caught the bus at the end of the street and headed to the town square. It was important to Caitlyn to discover why quilting had been a part of her Mother's life. Caitlyn stepped off the bus and waited for the light to change. The quilt shop had been a part of the main square shops for as long as she could remember. Caitlyn pushed the wooden door open, the jingle of the bell alerted everyone in the store another customer had entered. Caitlyn's eyes widened as every color in the universe stood in rows and stacks of cloth. The smell of the older building blended with the fresh new smell of material. She smiled as Miss. Irene walked towards her.

"Hello Caitlyn. Welcome to your Mothers world," Irene said and hugged Caitlyn.

"I never knew," She said.

"How about a Coke and we'll talk," Irene said.

"I'd really like that Miss. Irene," Caitlyn said. She followed the elderly woman and paused to observe the huge room filled with sewing machines. The ladies inside filled the room with talk, laughter, and beautiful creations to be cherished. Caitlyn recognized several ladies from their church. The two entered a small office where boxes of material were stacked almost to the ceiling.

"Did you look at the quilts?" Irene asked.

"No, ma'am," Caitlyn said.

Irene frowned and motioned for Caitlyn to sit down.

"There are three completed quilts. They will be given to each of you, on your wedding day. The quilt for Cierra's is incomplete," Irene said.

"Oh no," Caitlyn said.

"Your Mother began to make Cierra's, but became too ill to finish. She left it here. I intended to finish it, but haven't the time," Irene said. She handed a small bottle Coke to Caitlyn.

Caitlyn took a drink and cleared her throat.

"Do you think you could teach me how to quilt?" Caitlyn asked.

Irene smiled. "I think that can be arranged."

Caitlyn returned home from the shop. She walked directly to the attic and looked at each quilt. They were all the same. A beautiful appliquéd yellow rose in the middle of each quilt with designs that surrounded it. Caitlyn discovered cards addressed to each daughter. She wanted to open the envelope addressed to her, but would wait until the appropriate time. Caitlyn replaced the quilts and cards to the cedar chest. She would learn to quilt and complete the gift her Mother began for Cierra.

"Caitlyn, Caitlyn!" Cierra called.

"I'm sorry. I was just thinking of all the things I have left to do," Caitlyn said.

"Does the dress fit me?" Cierra asked.

"It's perfect," Caitlyn answered.

Cierra was the last of the sister's to be married. Each time one sister was married a quilt would be given two days before the wedding. Cierra never knew of the quilts as the meeting was between married sister and bride to be. Each new bride was sworn to secrecy in order not to spoil the meaning of the quilt. The individual cards spoke of love and hope for each daughter's future. Cierra's time had arrived. Two days before the wedding, the sisters met to honor their Mother and present the gift.

"Cierra this evening is very special," Caitlyn said.

"When you were five Caitlyn discovered a hope chest of quilts," Cathy said.

"Mother made one for each daughter," Caitlyn said.

"She had completed three quilts," Cindy added.

"Caitlyn discovered your unfinished quilt at Miss Irene's," Cathy continued.

"I learned to quilt. It was important for you to have the gift," Caitlyn said, and handed Cierra the box.

Cierra opened the card written by her Mother. The tears increased and caused streaks in her make-up. Her hands trembled as the ribbon was removed. Cierra removed the tissue and lifted the quilt from the box. She slowly ran her hand over the single yellow rose in the center. Cierra gently touched the detailed stitching.

"This is lovely," she said.

"Mother's love made it easy for me to finish," Caitlyn said.

A month later Caitlyn hung a photograph of the four sisters and their yellow rose quilts on her bedroom wall. She understood now, the reason her Mother needed to leave something tangible for each daughter. The hall clock began to chime. Caitlyn walked to the front door of her home.

"Mom, where are you going?" the young girl asked.

Caitlyn smiled at her daughter. "To Miss Irene's, my love."

About the Author

Janet Shawgo lives in Galveston Texas but over her twenty plus years as a travel nurse her life has crossed the United States.

Being a nurse for over thirty-three years, most of those in labor and delivery, has assisted in her writings. She starting writing in 2009 and has five books published to date.

Her *Look For Me* series has some thirty awards and acknowledgements. Janet has added some interest to her stories from her own travels. Research and actually putting feet on the ground helped to bring my stories to life.

Writing has become important to Janet. She has many stories running through her mind and cannot wait to share them with others.

About Houston Writers House

The goals of this organization are to facilitate those in the writing community to network and connect with others to achieve their publishing and marketing goals.

We are dedicated to helping writers improve their craft, build their brand, pinpoint their audience, and improve marketing skills. We support our authors, whether traditionally published or self-published, through critique groups, monthly socials, workshops and conferences providing varying topics from esteemed literary professionals.

Learn more at www.houstonwritershouse.net

Made in the USA
Middletown, DE
15 November 2024